FIVE DAYS
WITH A DUKE

Heart of a
Scandal
SERIES

CHRISTI
CALDWELL©

OTHER TITLES BY
CHRISTI CALDWELL

A NOTE FROM THE AUTHOR

Dear Readers,

I have to admit, there was a lot of sadness when I wrote The End of *Five Days With a Duke*. I had so much fun writing Constance and Connell's story. There were many times I found myself laughing aloud as I typed…and also sighing, at their romance. And yet, this book also marks The End of my *Heart of a Scandal* series. The five girls (Aldora, Rowena, Meredith, Emilia, and Constance) first to find the Heart of a Duke pendant are now all grown-up and each of their stories complete.

I hope you enjoy the last installment of The Heart of a Scandal series!!

Happy Reading!

Hugs,

Christi

PROLOGUE

Summer, 1822

TEN YEARS AGO, ALMOST TO the day, the Duke of Renaud had lost absolutely everything.

He'd inherited a recalcitrant ward and her illegitimate babe, and with the inherited responsibilities, he'd severed his relationship with the only woman he'd ever—or would ever—love.

He'd been certain there was no greater pain than letting his then-betrothed go, and all to look after the brand-new babe of a distant woman he'd never met.

He'd wanted the pair of them gone and his betrothed back and just they two in the world.

Only to find on the almost-anniversary of their arrival in his life, in an ultimate twist of irony, he'd been wrong on every single score.

Frozen at the floor-to-ceiling windowpane, his hands clasped low behind his back, Connell stared blankly out. Not directly at the party below. But rather, just over the gathering to the ornate watering fountain set within the lone patch of grass upon the graveled drive.

A trio, rendered specks by the distance of his window to the ground, remained within his line of vision. That small happy group, along with the sea of footmen and maids that formed a neat half circle around them. They could go to hell.

The whole lot of them.

Nay, not all of them.

His gaze went to the small figure, and at his back, his fingers tightened reflexively, surely leaving nail marks he didn't feel.

She stood sandwiched between her glowing mother... and a stranger. The man who'd sired Iris, who'd returned, and now would just take her away.

It didn't matter to him that it was the other man's legal right. And even worse, even more selfishly, it didn't matter that this reunion was what both his ward and her daughter had wished for. For Connell *was* selfish. For Iris and Hazel, he'd given up his life. He'd given up his former love. He'd reshaped his very existence... only to lose them?

The safer, familiar anger that had fueled him and sustained him since the other man's reappearance roared to life.

The moment Hazel and Iris boarded that carriage and took off down the damned drive, he never wanted to see the pair of them again.

As if she'd heard that silent vow and recognized it for the lie it was, Iris tipped her chubby face up. Her eyes landed on Connell's spot.

Her earlier exuberance dipped and dimmed, and the evidence of her sadness had the same effect as a lash upon his heart.

Releasing his arms, he moved closer to the window and lifted his palms, waving in the unique "hello" Iris had done as a babe and continued on through her almost eleven years.

Iris' smile was instantly restored, the one that dimpled her cheek. He could never deny her anything when she turned it on him. In a matched gesture, she wagged her fingers.

Her father said something, and as quick as if the moment had never been, she dropped her arm and spun to face the tall, too-thin gent. And just like that, Connell, with his hand still up, was forgotten.

Tears filled his throat, and the control he'd managed this morn snapped. He squeezed his eyes tight and fixed on breathing, because if he gave in to the sorrow of what he'd lost—who he'd lost—he'd never recover.

He'd thought losing Emilia Aberdeen was a pain he'd never recover from. For in the immediacy of that breakup, it had been impossible to fathom being any more brokenhearted.

Only to find just how bloody wrong he'd been.

This moment here and now would be what shattered him completely. Strangling on a sob, Connell sagged and caught the low window frame to keep from crumbling to his knees. Using the hard oak as a crutch, he pulled himself sideways so that his back rested alongside the wall, and his misery was hidden from the happy party below.

Catching his long hair between his fingers, he tugged the strands, wanting to feel any kind of pain other than the one that ravaged him.

Thump. Thump. Thump.

He'd come to think of those exaggerated, heavy footfalls as his butler Addlington's calling card the past fortnight since Connell's world had fallen apart. Then would come the rhythmic knock.

Knock-pause-knock-scratch.

And lastly—

"*Ahem.*"

What in hell could the servant possibly want? Why wasn't he outside even now with the happy send-off party, and Iris and her mother, and the bastard of a father—

"I said, ahe—"

"I heard you," he bellowed. "What in the hell do you want?"

Which the other man apparently took to mean *enter.*

At the slight click of the handle, Connell scrambled upright and dashed his hands over his eyes. When Addlington entered, Connell had placed himself as he'd been at the window, in his earlier pose constructed of feigned nonchalance.

"Shouldn't you be belowstairs?" he asked tersely the moment the butler's visage appeared in the immaculate, gleaming crystal panel. Having joined Connell's staff near the time he'd broken off his betrothal, Addlington had been with the family since Iris had arrived. Countless times, Connell had caught the little girl in the company of the butler. As such, he was not so self-absorbed that he didn't recognize Addlington would feel keenly the cheerful girl's departure.

"Yes. Yes, I should, Your Grace." Addlington paused. "But then, I thought that you should, as well."

"You're insolent, and I should sack you."

"Yes, undoubtedly you should." The servant paused. "And as I'm already being insolent, if I may also say?"

"I'd rather you didn't," he said coolly.

Addlington went on as if he hadn't spoken. "If you do not go and make your goodbyes to the little miss, you'll regret it, Your Grace."

The crystal pane acted as a mirror, and staring back from within was the bitter twist of Connell's lips.

Regret.

An apt word to capture much of what Connell carried through life. Regret. There was so damned much of it. So many mistakes made. So many faulty missteps and decisions, ones that had been made with the greatest of intentions.

But abandoning his spot high above the happy gathering below and watching as Iris and her mother departed, leaving only silence and memories in their wake? Nay, his well-meaning butler was wrong on that score—Connell wouldn't be one ounce sorry for failing to take part in that celebratory departure. "Your concern is noted," Connell murmured, resuming his study of the watering fountain below. "If you would close the door behind you?"

Addlington hesitated. "As you wish, Your Grace." Taking several flourishing backward steps, the butler reached for the handle.

"Addlington?" he called.

The man of like years stopped. "Your Grace?"

"You should, however, join… " Connell fought to get the beloved name out… and failed. "The gathering," he settled for instead.

"Thank you, Your Grace."

Connell made as if he'd not heard that expression of gratitude. He didn't want it. He wasn't deserving of it. Rather, it was for her—little Iris, who'd always loved Addlington.

The heavily carved, oak panel stared back in the glass, the only indication that the butler had gone and Connell was again alone.

For the first time… ever.

Once upon a lifetime ago, when he'd been a young man out of university, there'd been lovers and mistresses and friends… until he'd fallen in love, and every day had been consumed with Emilia Aberdeen. After the end of their betrothal, there had been only Iris and her flighty, but always smiling mother.

The driver came forward and drew the pink lacquer door open.

First, into the carriage went Hazel.

Iris, however, lingered. Addlington, who must have taken flight for the speed with which he'd made it to the little girl's side, knelt beside her.

Iris flung herself into the butler's arms, staggering the servant.

It was too much.

Squeezing his eyes closed, Connell stepped away from the window. He'd not survive this. It would be easier to lop off a limb than lose a girl who was like his own child. More than ten years of raising her, loving her, only to have her father reappear as if none of those years had ever mattered.

But then, they didn't.

Not truly.

Because she'd always belonged to another. Connell had just never imagined a world in which that man would realize the gift he'd lost, or that he'd return and take with him all of Connell's existence.

The distant click of the carriage door closing brought Connell's eyes flying open. Hurrying back into position, he stared on, motionless, as the conveyance rolled along, rocking and swaying. He stared on until the garish pink vehicle diminished in size and then ultimately faded beyond the horizon, leaving a marked finality in its absence.

Now, there was no one.

There'd be no play tea parties, or midnight snacking, or Maypole festivities.

Yes, there was no one.

He hardened his jaw.

And Connell was determined that there would never be anyone, ever again.

Around that same time, in London

LADY CONSTANCE BRANDLEY WEPT.

Nay, more specifically, she blubbered. Great, big, blustery, snorting tears, the sound of them made all the more pronounced and obscene for the barrenness of the rooms filled with nothing but the echoes of her misery.

It was silly.

She'd lost so much.

They were just things.

That was what she'd told herself each and every time some scrap had been carted off.

That was what she'd believed with her whole heart. She had a mother and a father, though stuffy, who loved her. They weren't a caricature of evil parents attempting to marry her off to save their finances.

And given that her younger brother had been missing for these past several years, it really was an outrageously ridiculous thing for Constance to cry over.

And yet, mayhap that was why she cried, because it was just a reminder of a far greater loss.

I don't care what Mama and Papa say. I think you play beautifully, and well, you never much cared what they said, either way.

Her brother's words echoed in her mind. He'd been the younger, underfoot brother, but on that day, he'd defended her... and encouraged her to continue playing.

"And h-he is gone," she whispered through her tears into the quiet. Just as her instrument was.

It had been inevitable that her parents would go and touch the music room—but it had meant so very much to her.

For when other young ladies—her friends, strangers, everyone her age—had gone off and married and then went on to fill up their nurseries, Constance had felt pangs of yearning for what they had, but at the same time, she'd found a great contentment in the life she did have... in playing.

As long as a lady had a cello, one didn't require a man.

That had been the motto she'd written within the folds of her diary and the one she'd come to believe.

The cello spoke for her when she had something to say.

Angrily dashing at her eyes, Constance touched her gaze around the bare, gilded walls. The floral paintings made upon the wallpaper lent an air of pretend opulence that was belied by the faded rectangles where golden-framed mirrors had once hung. That corner where the harp had sat was now empty. The rug at the center of the room, where the pianoforte had taken up a central place, was gone, along with the grand instrument that had occupied a place upon it. Through a new sheen of tears, she looked to the place alongside the row of windows overlooking the stables below. Sunlight cascaded through the dusty glass panels, damnably cheerful, with three rays forming a triumvirate of sunlight that showered upon the place her cello had once rested.

Her body shook, and she bit her lip hard to keep the tears at bay.

Only, there was no one here. Her parents were gone for the morn, playing the expert roles they'd mastered of nonimpoverished lord and lady.

Nor would anyone else dare visit the Brandleys' music room.

Though, to be more precise, no one was to be shown to any room but one in the Brandleys' household—the Blue Parlor.

With that, Constance gave in to her misery.

Rolling onto her side, Constance curled her arms around her knees and wept all the harder. The ugly kind of tears that shook her body until her stomach muscles and chest ached from the violent paroxysms, but the pain was welcome.

There'd been no great love of a man, as three of her friends had known. There was no husband. And because of that, no children. And that had been all right. Constance had made peace with the fact that she'd not had the love of a gentleman… because she'd had another love—her cello.

Her cello, that magnificent instrument that had always been there, allowing her to escape to the songs within her head.

Constance wept until her tears faded to a shuddery hiccoughing.

With her cheek pressed against the cool, hard floor, she lay there, staring off, allowing herself this one moment to break down before she was forced to pick herself up, plaster on a smile, and live the lie of all lies.

Footsteps from somewhere in the house reached her ears.

Though, in actuality, all footsteps were magnified now. *All* sound was amplified in the empty household.

For now, she was absolutely safe in her misery.

Or she *should* have been.

For now, however, proved as short-lived as the Brandleys' wealth.

The ungreased doors squealed loudly as they were opened.

Prone on the floor, Constance went absolutely motionless.

Oh, bloody hell.

The last thing she wished was to be discovered by her mother or father. Not in this way.

"The Marchioness of Mulgrave," the old family butler, Scott, intoned from the doorway.

She'd been wrong. The last thing Constance wished was to be discovered by any one of her friends. No matter how dear they were or how long she'd known them.

Oh, bloody, bloody hell.

"Thank you, Scott." All attempts at forced cheer were hopelessly ruined by the ragged roughness of a voice hoarse from all the tears she'd cried. "That will be all," she said, propelling herself to an upright position with all the aplomb she could muster.

"As you wish, Lady Constance."

What she wished was to have Scott honor the rules and requirements of showing guests—even beloved friend-guests— only to the Blue Parlor.

Alas…

They'd been found out.

It had been only a matter of time.

After all, a secret couldn't stay a secret. Not really. And not forever.

But it could have been a good deal worse. Their scandalous circumstances could have been discovered by mercenary strangers rather than her closest friend in the world.

Constance took a moment to wipe the remnants of tears from her eyes and cheeks. Wiping them once more for good measure, she stood and faced Emilia.

Alas, she needn't have worried about composing herself.

Emilia's shocked gaze was fixed not on Constance, but on the cavernous and very bare music room. "My goodness," Lady Emilia whispered. Her horrified pronouncement rang all the louder in the empty room.

Lady Constance Brandley's dearest friend was taking the discovery a good deal better than she would have expected.

"It's not really as bad as all that," Constance lied. And oh, did she lie. Most of the furniture had been sold to cover debts. With the exception of familial portraits, every last painting had been tugged from the walls and sent on to auction. The vases and knickknacks and Aubusson carpets and throws. Her gaze slid to the row of windows, and sadness threatened to choke her. The music room had been emptied, too.

Emilia blinked slowly, and Constance knew the moment her always-in-control friend had found her footing. "How long?"

"Not long," she lied. Again.

Emilia sharpened her too-clever eyes on Constance's face. "How long?" her friend repeated, perfectly enunciating each syllable.

"Perhaps four years or so?" Six. It had been six, almost to the date. However, four felt a good deal less sizable than six.

Reaching behind her, Emilia grabbed the door handles and drew the panels closed. "Constance," she said gently.

Sinking onto the floor in a swoosh of skirts, Constance drew her knees close and sighed. "Six years."

Emilia cursed. "*Siiix*?" Her friend joined Constance, struggling a bit as she lowered herself onto the scuffed parquet floor.

"You shouldn't," she said quickly.

"I'm carrying a babe," Emilia said dryly. "I'm not infirm." The expectant mother laid a tender palm on her lightly rounded belly.

Another pang struck close to Constance's heart. A different one from her earlier mourning. Not for the missing cello, but for the babes she'd never have. And Constance hated herself for envying the other woman any of her happiness. Having been jilted, her heart broken by a heartless cad of a duke, Emilia had found love and deserved any joy that life brought her.

"What happened?" Emilia asked.

Constance rested her cheek along the fabric of one of last year's gowns. "I… don't know. I've always been rubbish with numbers, and as such, I've not been able to make sense of the finances, other than to know my father has accumulated outstanding debts." The maze of debts somehow connected to her brother's travels. They'd always supported his pursuits, but there'd been an increased urgency to the payments Father made.

And in the end, Constance's passions had gone to fund them. Bitterness sat on her tongue like vinegar.

Emilia laid a hand on hers. "What can I do to help?"

"Nothing," she said automatically. She'd not take handouts. Nor would she sell herself into marriage in the name of money either. Which, in short, left a lady with few options.

"Is there anything?"

"It is fine."

Her friend lightly squeezed her fingers. "That is not what I asked."

"It will work out," she assured. It had to. It always did. They'd been without for so long, and they'd got on just as long.

But something this morning *felt* different. Mayhap the gravity of her family's situation hadn't hit Constance before because she hadn't lost anything she truly loved… until today.

Emilia inched closer and opened her mouth to speak, but then stopped. Her friend stole a glance over her shoulder at the closed doors. "I'm certain that when you say you are 'fine' that you indeed are. Be that as it may, if you were interested in"—she lowered her already quiet voice to a hushed whisper that Constance strained to hear—"earning modest funds, I might have an idea for you."

An opportunity to earn her own funds? She could purchase back her cello.

"It would only be a temporary post, but I believe, if you're successful at it, I may be able to coordinate—"

"I'll take it," she blurted. There were no certainties about the future. What Constance did know was that she wanted her cello back, and Emilia had presented her with the opportunity to secure the means to do so. "What is 'it'?"

Emilia smiled slowly, her grin stretching from ear to ear. "Well, you see, I've kept a secret through the years."

Constance leaned forward, hanging on her friend's words. "No one knows, and no one can know… for either of our sake." And with that, the other woman proceeded to explain.

CHAPTER 1

Winter, 1823
London, England

THE EMBROIDERED BOMBAZINE CURTAINS HAD been hung in the Earl and Countess of Tipden's parlor with meticulous care.

Though, in fairness, the curtains really were hung with care in *every* room of the Earl of Tipden's palatial townhouse.

However, the Countess of Tipden's meticulous tastes and luxuriant styles did not account for that careful hanging.

Rather, the bare rooms absolutely merited it. After all, to toss them wide would lay open the greatest of Society's secrets—the Tipdens didn't have two sovereigns to rub together. Why, they didn't have a farthing to their name. The riches and wealth the *ton* believed they had, they in fact didn't have and never had.

Now, that had been the greatest and most impressive bit to the charade they'd managed to pull off.

What the Brandleys possessed in spades, however, was the skill of *pretending*. "If only one could furnish a home with that skill," Constance muttered. For then the Brandleys would have a palace to rival the king's.

"What was that, dear?" the countess called from that coveted spot beside the always well-regulated hearth. Never too much kindling. But also enough to cast heat to those seated closest to it. As if to highlight that very point, a wind battered the windowpanes, deepening the chill in the room.

"Nothing," Constance replied. "Nothing at all."

Alas, with her head bent over the same threadbare scrap she embroidered upon, the countess was firmly engrossed once more in that tedious-to-Constance-but-blissful-to-her-mother-task that occupied the older woman. If the world had bothered to look close enough.

Not even the older ladies her mother called dearest friends had seen.

Just one had.

As it had proven, the *right* someone had.

The memory of her end-of-summer exchange brought Constance back to the task at hand.

Seated on the hard bench of the once upholstered window seat, Constance reached for the note on top of the neatly tied, sizable stacks of letters. If the countess thought there was anything peculiar in the sudden influx of mail Constance received, she'd been contented with the explanation some months ago—that they were a product of Emilia, who'd recently had her babe.

Sliding the slightly dull tip of her pencil under the seal, she opened the envelope.

Constance unfolded the missive.

Dear Mrs. Matcher,

A dukedom, as I know you're aware, is the rarest of the titles, with only a handful of those gentlemen eligible for marriage. As such, I wish to receive your estimable guidance on how to earn the title of duchess.

With deepest appreciation and greatest of respect...

Constance's face pulled, and without bothering to read the initials at the bottom of the missive, she folded the letter and set it down hard as the first of a pile for the questions she'd not reply to.

"Has Lady Emilia written you with distressing information?" her mother asked, bringing Constance's head whipping up.

Given the lack of perceptiveness the countess had demonstrated these years, that was the last question Constance would have expected. As it was, the older woman's gaze was reserved for her embroidery frame.

"No. No," she assured. "Everything is quite fine." As fine as all could be, given their financial state and Constance's distressing efforts with Mrs. Matcher's column. "She was simply lamenting the cold winter weather."

"Bah, the winter weather has been a boon to us, Constance."

"Oh, yes, it's been particularly helpful in the heating of the rooms," she said drolly.

Her mother frowned. "In case you've not been able to deduce from the empty hearth, that isn't at all true. Quite the opposite, really."

As if on cue, a sharp winter's wind battered at the windows. The curtains did little to mute the blast of cold that penetrated the ancient lead panes.

Alas, the countess was never much one for detecting sarcasm.

Her teeth chattering, Constance drew the shawl she'd already double-folded close, burrowing into the threadbare velvet lining.

Nay, she well knew that winters had been best for her family. For at that dreary, gray time of year, everyone took themselves off to their country seats, and it was only then when the Brandleys were spared the worry of the *ton* discovering their greatest kept secret—the Brandleys were impoverished.

The discovery was inevitable, as Emilia's arrival at the end of the summer had proven.

But for now, all the Brandleys had was their pride and the hope that they could keep their secret...

Returning to her work, Constance gathered up another note.

Dearest Mrs. Matcher,

Trust me when I begin this note by assuring you I'm not a lady driven by wealth and title and power above all else.

"That is encouraging," she muttered under her breath.

"What is that, dear?"

"Nothing, Mother. I'm simply speaking to myself."

The countess frowned and lowered her tray. "No, you're not. You're speaking to me."

"Yes. Yes. Now. But before, I was..." She sighed. "Never mind."

"As you wish, dear." The countess proceeded to hum to herself as she stitched away.

Constance sighed. She required an office. There was nothing else for it. How was a woman, after all, supposed to conduct any meaningful work—particularly work that was meant to be secret and confidential—from a shared parlor space with her mother? Shaking out her page, she lifted it once more and picked up reading where she'd left off.

However, in the spirit of absolute honesty, Mrs. Matcher, I find myself confessing that I am searching for something very specific where love and marriage are concerned. I'm searching for the heart of a duke.

"Oh, bloody hell," she whispered.

"What is it now?"

"Nothing," she said automatically, not taking her gaze from the elegant scrawl and the three initials inked at the bottom of the page.

All the requests and questions about earning the affections of a duke... was that all women truly wished for? Was it all they desired? Giving her head a disgusted shake, Constance abandoned the note atop the other in the discard pile and reached for another.

Quickly unfolding it, she proceeded to read. This note was written in a slightly less meticulous hand than the ones to proceed it.

Miserable in Mayfair

Dear Mrs. Matcher,

In the spirit of fairness, I shall be very straightforward with you.

This again.

My former guardian has the ugliest of reputations.

Constance sat up quickly.

"Something interesting in your note, Constance?"

Yes. "No," she said in a bid to head off any further commentary from her mother.

He's not well-thought of by nearly anyone in Society, but he was my guardian and lovingly raised me, but then when it was time for me to leave him, he became quite sad.

Constance's heart squeezed, and she brought the page closer to her face, riveted by each heartbreaking word so neatly scrawled about the lonely lord. "Poor man," she whispered.

And yet, I fear if I give you his identity, you will refuse.

Her intrigue stirred.

But, Miss Matcher, he is lonely and very much in need of finding love. Please help. If you're willing, he is located at 17 Mayfair Lane in

London.

Signed,

Concerned in Leeds

Constance reread the note once more, this request so very different from every other, many of which had been compelled by avarice and greed. This one was written out of love and concern.

And yet, her work as Mrs. Matcher wasn't a matchmaking business. It was an advice column.

Constance drummed her fingertips on the letter.

But why could it not be both? Hadn't that all but been Emilia's advice when she'd passed on the temporary assignment? Mayhap Constance could help the lonely, sad old guardian find happiness and also include that journey in her column. Excitement built in her chest. It would be something Emilia had never done. Nay, it would be something no one had ever done in any London paper, something uniquely her own that would no doubt captivate Society.

Holding up an imaginary quill, she trailed her fingertips through the air.

Five Ways to Make a Duke Find Love in London.

Of course, the readers needn't know the gentleman wasn't, in fact, a duke, but rather a doddering lord whose ward had gone and married. The letters she'd received were all proof enough that dukes were what sold. And there was the matter of protecting the real subject's identity.

"What are you doing, Constance?"

Constance hastily dropped her hand to her lap and looked over at her mother, who was fully engrossed in her embroidery. "I'm stretching my hand," she said, the lie rolling all too easily from her tongue. Having gotten into all manner of mischief as a girl, she'd easily acquired the ability to prevaricate where the countess was concerned.

Free of her mother's attentions, Constance redirected her focus to the Lonely Lord. A meeting. She'd require a meeting with him. And then, once she met the old peer, she might determine just what he was looking for in love. Because no one was too old to find love.

Nor did that view come from the fact that she was now thirty herself, a spinster on the shelf, with nary a suitor in… eight years now.

It had been eight years.

The more she thought of herself and her circumstances and how very much they paralleled the young lady's guardian, her excitement grew.

After all, there were far more people such as her and this old lord, alone, deserving of love and happiness and…

She went stock-still and then sprang to the edge of her seat.

That is my column!

That would be what set Constance's apart from what Emilia's had been…

It was what the world needed, and needed desperately. Happily-ever-afters and love for all, including those who'd lost the first bloom of youth.

Not that at thirty, she was the same as the wizened nobleman who'd shuttered himself away from the world.

But neither were they completely dissimilar.

With a smile, Constance gathered her pen and prepared for her meeting with the Lonely Lord.

CHAPTER 2

CONNELL HATED LONDON.

As such, it was to be his penance, living here. In a vomit-inducing pink stucco townhouse, no less.

London carried memories of his youth, of the carefree, roguish gentleman he'd been who'd abandoned his scoundrel ways when he'd fallen in love.

This place, however—he'd purchased it but a month ago—contained no memories. Why, it barely contained the essential furnishings. As such, living here was a good deal better than living in hell, which there could be no doubting the now empty Gladden Manor had, in fact, become.

His feet kicked up on the edge of the windowsill, Connell drew deep of his pipe and welcomed the smoke that filled his lungs.

This time, he didn't have to fight back the images or memories of Iris and her mother. Connell had become such an expert on it that the mere thought of their names didn't usher in a single thing aside from the numbness that had found a welcome home inside.

He exhaled a small circle of white. He tapped the ash over the side of his chair and onto the floor.

"Making a mess, you are, an' who do ye expect cleans that, Yar Grace?"

Bored as he was by everything in life, he glanced to the entrance of the empty library and found the scowling housekeeper, Jennie, one of but two servants he'd acquired—and entirely by chance.

Not bothering to wait for an invitation, the birdlike woman stomped over. She wrinkled her nose. "From the smell o' that stuff, it canna be good for ye," she scolded.

"I trust the brandy I've caught you nipping would somehow be better for me, then?" he drawled.

Jennie grunted. "Dunno wot yar talking about." Guilt splotched the old woman's cheeks, making her out as the liar she was.

"Of course you don't," he said drolly. This time, however, when he tipped his ashes, he knocked them into the porcelain vase near his seat.

The day Iris and her mother left, Connell had ordered his man of affairs to purchase a residence far away from his country seat that could be moved into as quickly as possible. And if it was staff-less, the better it was. He'd wanted to shut an unfamiliar door on the whole world and suffer on with only his own miserable self for company.

Only to find upon his arrival a fortnight ago Jennie and James—husband-and-wife squatters comfortably ensconced in the townhouse. "Rapscallion, ye are."

And for the unconventionality of a pair that had a taste for Connell's fine French spirits, he found himself preferring their honest, not-hovering company to the usual houseful of servants he'd had at every estate or townhouse he'd ever resided in. As such, he was in no haste to fill the house with men and women scurrying about to see to his needs.

"Ah'm to take me nap. Anything else ye be wantin'?"

That had proven the greatest of oddities in his short time here. The servants informing him about how they intended to spend their time and just what services they'd render or not render. In a way that would have horrified Connell's late parents, he rather found himself enjoying that insolence.

He waved a hand. "Off with you."

Of course, he needn't have bothered with an acknowledgment. The old woman, with her white, greasy hair, had already started for the door.

And Connell was left... alone.

Blessedly, happily, and quite contentedly... *alone.*

Once more.

Sprawling on his back, he clamped the stem of his pipe between his teeth. Overhead, a pastel country scene stared back, mocking him with its cheerfulness.

Everything about the place was so damned cheerful. "Even the damned murals," he muttered as he exhaled a cloud of white toward that disgusting scene.

A bright-eyed little girl with voluminous blonde curls and plump cheeks sat between a couple, a lady with a wide-brimmed hat and a jacketless gent, who smiled adoringly at each other over the top of the child's head.

He stared intently at the little girl. He didn't blink, just took in the bucolic scene.

Not long ago, he'd had that.

Or, as close as he would ever come to that simple happiness.

There'd been laughter and mischief and always a household full of cheer.

Connell raised one of his middle fingers at that trio, and with the other hand, he raised his pipe to his lips and let the smoke fill his lungs. After finishing it off, Connell turned the pipe over and dropped the remnants of his smoke into the nearby vase.

He narrowed his eyes on the porcelain piece.

Connell squinted. By God, if it wasn't that same damned trio frolicking on his ceiling, enjoying a ride upon a garden swing. Was there nothing that painted group did not do?

For sale. He was going to sell every cock-a-hoop item in this damned household. And paint. He was going to have the front stucco scrubbed of all joviality and the interior walls splashed with some sterile white wallpaper.

Closing his eyes, he soon fell asleep.

A distant banging penetrated Connell's slumber. He forced tired eyes open and struggled to gain his bearings in the chilled room.

The room and everything about it was foreign.

Not even a fire had been set or stoked in the hearth? Why wasn't there warmth? Iris would be chilled.

And then it all came rushing back to him.

Iris… who was gone. Who'd been lost to him. That loss came as fresh as when her mother had informed him of her plans to marry the bounder who'd first deserted her. Through the fog of pain and haze of confusion, he glanced around.

Where in blazes was…?

His gaze collided with… the merry vase at his feet. Stifling a curse, he turned the damned article around.

Of course.

The happy family, painted on the opposite side, stared back. Taunting him. Jeering him for his misery and loneliness and—

Knock-knock-knock.

Or his *previous* loneliness. For now, it would appear as though he had company.

What in hell?

That was… preposterous. Who would be pounding at his door? Be it when he'd been away in Kent or here in London, no one visited him. Not any longer. After he'd traded his bachelor ways for those of a responsible guardian, the other gentlemen he'd called "friends" had found other bounders without responsibilities for company. And the respectable guests had stopped coming 'round after Connell had broken his betrothal, which had left simply… no one else to pay him calls. Either way, his servants would see to whoever was on his doorstep.

Knock-knock-knock.

His derelict servants would not be seeing to anything. In fact, they were likely two sheets to the wind and well on the first legs of their morning or afternoon—or whatever time of day it was—nap they habitually stole.

Cursing roundly, Connell swung his legs over the sides of the sofa and set his feet on the floor. The cold immediately penetrated his thick silk stockings. By the time he made the march through the confoundingly unfamiliar residence, the knocking had come to a stop.

Splendid. Whoever the hell had come was now gone, and he could enjoy the pleasure of his solitary company.

Pain jolted through him, and he came to an abrupt stop, ironically upon that odious ball of sunshine that adorned the middle of the white marble foyer.

For so long, his days had been filled with daily picnics and games of hide-and-go-seek.

And now, what was there?

A drink. He needed a drink.

Connell turned to go… when through the thin glass panel along the side of the door, he caught a glimpse of a lone figure on his stoop.

He peered through the translucent gossamer fabric at the odd creature.

What in blazes?

Like Lady Jersey without the benefit of her quizzing glass, the woman squinted, and then under the enormous brim of her feathered bonnet, she cupped her hands over her eyes. "Whoohooloo, I see you."

The enormous slab of oak managed to mute, but not silence, his guest's voice.

Though, *intruder* would be a more apt and fitting term for the one with her face all but pressed to his newly acquired windowpane. There was certainly no one he was expecting. No one even knew of his recent acquisition.

The woman stuck her nose against the glass. "If you'd be so kind and open the door?"

And it happened. For the first time in the six months since Iris had gone, Connell was intrigued. It'd been so long since he'd felt anything but a numbness that he'd believed himself incapable of feeling… well, anything but annoyance anymore.

"I have business with your employer," the stranger was saying.

Business with his employer? She'd mistaken him for a servant. But then, it was a fair enough mistake to make given that generally every last Mayfair residence had these doors opened by either a first or second butler. Connell, however, was certainly the only duke without the benefit of either.

Stalking forward, he grabbed the handle and opened the door. The woman immediately stopped speaking. "Oh," she blurted, and with horror rapidly filling her eyes, she looked him up and down. "You… are not old or wizened."

Connell rubbed at sleep-bleary eyes. There was something vaguely familiar about the pleasingly plump, red-cheeked miss standing on his stoop. "Should I be?" He searched his foggy mind in a bid to place those perfectly rounded cheeks.

"Yes," she exclaimed.

And those pretty blue eyes, albeit angry eyes. And her lips. Lush and perfectly plump on the bottom and slightly thinner on the top, they weren't lips a man should or would forget. Only, the flat line of those lips proved to be the identifier. He groaned. Her! As in Lady Caroline or Lady Con… something or another. Whatever her name, she was none other than his former betrothed's best friend. Or one of them.

"Is this some kind of damned dream?" He was being haunted by Lady Emilia's friends. This was to be further punishment for breaking that betrothal, then.

CHAPTER 3

CONSTANCE CAME TO ANY NUMBER of realizations, and all at once.

One, the object of her pity wasn't, in fact, an old, sad, lonely guardian, but rather, a surly, glaring gentleman.

Two, the poor man wasn't at all poor, either in his financial or his emotional state.

And three, she needn't have worried herself in lying to readers. The gentleman was very much… a duke. As in the Duke of Renaud. Who'd stolen the heart of Constance's dearest friend, Emilia, and then broken it when he'd ended their betrothal.

"You," she seethed.

The Duke of Renaud gave her an icy once-over. "Given that you're the one barging into my household, I daresay if either of us is entitled to indignant surprise, it should be me."

Indignant surprise indeed.

As if he were the wounded party. Not that *she* was the wounded party. That courtesy belonged to Emilia. Not that Emilia wasn't blissfully happy and hopelessly in love with her devoted husband. That was neither here nor there. Nay, the Duke of Renaud was no wounded party.

What he was, was a miserable, heartless scoundrel. "Well, if it is a dream, Your Grace, then we are both having the same blasted one, and I certainly wouldn't classify it as a dream, but rather, a bloody nightmare."

He whistled. "The mouth on you."

"Thank you." After all, certain situations merited sass. "And given your sudden concern with propriety, what are you doing answering your own door? Don't you have a butler?"

He bristled. "Of course I have a butler."

She peered around a pair of broad shoulders, searching—

The duke pulled the door closed even farther so that the slab hung open only a smidge, and her unhindered view into his household was cut off. "What the hell do you want, Lady Caroline?"

"Constance." The bounder. He'd been betrothed to her best friend and couldn't even remember her name? "My name is Constance."

"I don't care if you're Eve here to atone for your sins. What do you want?" he demanded, not at all the kindly old guardian she'd been seeking.

Well. "Forgive me," she said, matching his tones in coldness. "I'm afraid I've come to the wrong residence." Glancing down at her letter, she skimmed the contents. "I am looking for—"

Click. The decisive sound of the wood panel closing brought Constance's head whipping up. She gasped. Why… why… the bounder had just shut the door in her face.

Click. Constance grunted as the lock turned. *And* he'd locked it.

"Well, you needn't worry." She waved a fist at the fierce lion door-knocker. The metal creature hung with its mouth open midroar, as surly as the beast who dwelt within that residence. "The last person I was looking for was you." Looking for the address once more, Constance confirmed the number.

Seventeen.

With that number echoing in her head, she marched down the steps and looked at the neighboring townhouses. And then, with a horrible dread, she glanced up at the last doors she'd ever intentionally seek out.

"Seventeen," she said aloud, her breath making a little cloud of white in the cold.

Her stomach sank.

There'd been no mistake. This *was* her intended destination, after all.

But… but if not the address, there was surely a mistake somewhere. Why, writing Constance that note, appealing to her pity, and managing to lure her to a gentleman's residence? Someone had certainly played some manner of game with her.

She'd long committed the words upon the letter to memory, but the situation merited another read.

And yet, I fear if I give you his identity, you will refuse. But, Miss Matcher, he is lonely and very much in need of finding love.

Constance sighed. Yes, nothing in the note mentioned anything about an old lord. She had simply made assumptions based on what she'd read. Huddling in her cloak, she stole another look at the pink stucco townhouse.

She'd not taken the Duke of Renaud as a pink-stucco-townhouse manner of gentleman.

Even in their youths, back when Constance had known him through his association with Emilia, he'd always been attired in dark garments and shown a meticulous style for anything... well, not pink or frothy or light.

Not that there was anything frothy or light about the duke's character this day.

Constance stomped back toward her carriage, waiting at the end of the street.

The Duke of Renaud was surlier than she recalled.

Nay, the only recollections she had of him went back to when he'd been betrothed to Emilia, and in those days, His Grace had never been without a smile or a laugh.

Constance slowed her steps and then stopped altogether several feet from the carriage. She absently registered the driver climbing down from his box and pulling the door open in anticipation of her arrival.

Constance remained fixed to the pavement. Wind tugged at her skirts, the cool bite of winter air penetrating the heavy fabrics.

Despite her immediate conclusion that the letter to Mrs. Matcher had been made in jest, Constance racked her brain for what Emilia had confided in her about that long-ago breakup with His Grace, the Duke of Renaud. There'd been a ward and a child, but the age of the child Constance knew not, nor had Emilia mentioned that particular detail.

Reaching inside her reticule, Constance fished out the note

and carefully examined the scrawl. She noted other details that had previously escaped her: the slightly too big loping letters, the flourish of the hand, the small flower drawn at the bottom, which, well, Constance hadn't paid all that much attention to. Now, however, each and every sign pointed to the fact that the letter had been written by the young girl.

A young girl who was most concerned about the fact that she'd left her former guardian and his current sad state.

"It is a sad state." Just not in the way the young girl had meant.

"What is that, miss?"

She looked up at the graying servant who still stood in wait with the door held open.

"Nothing."

Closing her eyes, Constance went back and forth in her mind, fighting with herself, fighting with logic. She opened her eyes.

"Miss?" Whitey questioned.

Oh, hell and biscuits. "I'll be back in a moment." Turning on her heel, Constance started a march back down the pavement, along the same path she'd traveled.

What are you doing? What are you doing? What are you doing?

Her footfalls came in time to that five-syllable intonation.

She came to a stop outside Number Seventeen.

Collecting her hem, she took the steps and then grabbed the duke's angry lion and brought the banger down.

The door was opened almost immediately.

He'd either been lingering in the foyer or... nay, he'd been lingering. No one would have opened the door that quickly.

"*Youuu,*" he said in pained tones.

"May I?"

"I'd rather you..."

Constance proceeded around him.

"Well, in that case, please," he said in droll tones, "*do* come in." He closed the door behind them and leaned against the panel. "Do you intend to stay? Should I have guest rooms readied?"

Rooms readied? "Do not be ridiculous." She caught the mocking glint in his eyes. "*Hmph.* Well, surely you didn't expect we'd remain conversing on your stoop. It would be ruinous if I were to be discovered here."

The gentleman looped his arms at his chest. "But your paying an unmarried gentleman a call is quite aboveboard."

"Not at all." He'd always been a scoundrel. When Emelia had gone and fallen in love with the notorious rogue, the whole world had whispered that only ruin awaited. The duke had not changed one bit. "It's quite scandalous, really. My being here."

"I was being sarcastic," he said, his expression deadpan.

"Oh." Had he always had this biting wit? In their youth, she'd always been invisible to him, as was evidenced all these years later by the fact that he'd had no recollection of her name.

He lifted a golden brow, prompting Constance to clear her throat. "I've gone through the risks-to-reward analysis."

"Risks-to-reward analysis," he silently mouthed while she spoke.

"Given the whole of London is still gone for the winter, the risk of discovery, though perilous, remains small."

"*You* are here, Lady Cordelia," he pointed out.

"Constance. My name is…" It was really neither here nor there. "You are also here, my lord," she said, getting back to the reason for her being here.

"Your Grace."

Constance flashed an innocent smile. "Given you aren't one who much values a person's actual name, I trust you aren't all that particular on whether or not you're a 'Your Grace' or 'my lord.'"

His eyebrows drew sharply together.

Ignoring that palpable annoyance, Constance searched the spacious foyer. Her gaze landed on the ornate golden oak hall table. Taking a determined path across the pale pink marble floor, she set her bag down and then shoved her hood back so she could look without hindrance at the sad state of the duke's household.

The duke blanched. "My God, you *are* staying."

"Yes," she murmured as she took in his residence. "For the time being, anyway."

Despite the letter she'd received, there was nothing sad about the foyer. Quite the opposite. Having spent the past years living in a sparse household, with barely any trimmings or furniture, Constance had learned firsthand the true meaning behind a cold, sterile household. Cold floors bare of carpeting. Chilled, barren rooms devoid of cheer.

From the bucolic tableau of near-lifelike-in-size figures in the mural overhead, to the pale pink wallpaper and floors of a matching shade, one might even say the gentleman's residence was a visual antidote to the mere idea of sadness.

She lingered her stare upon the crystal sconces and the flecks of gold that sparkled in the wallpaper.

Nay, there was nothing sad about his residence. In fact, the entry alone oozed wealth and elegance.

"Have you concluded your study, my lady?"

"Of the household," she said, bringing her focus back to the real subject of her visit.

Miserable in Mayfair.

Though, in this moment, with the harsh slash of his hard lips and his flinty stare, the Duke of Renaud fit very much with the name his former ward had affixed to him in her letter.

That was when Constance knew, despite her initial reservations and her earlier resolve to leave, that she wasn't going anywhere. Not unlike her, the duke was very much in need, and they could very much help each other. Slowly peeling her gloves off, Constance deposited them in her cloak pocket. "There is still the matter of you."

There was still the matter of him?

"Me?"

The young lady nodded, confirming he'd not heard her wrong.

It did not, however, mean that her words still made any kind of sense.

"Given I'm here on a matter of business, might I suggest we adjourn to your offices, Your Grace?"

How had he failed to gather during his courtship of Lady Emilia that her closest friend in the world was as mad as a bedlamite? "You might suggest it, but it doesn't mean I'm taking you to my offices, my lady."

She frowned. "And here I'd not taken you for the stuffy sort who'd balk at meeting a young woman on a matter of business."

The whole damned reason he'd come to London was to be free of... well, everyone. It was why he'd sought out this damned townhouse, one that no one knew he was residing in. "We don't have business together," he snapped. He didn't want any manner of business with anyone. And that included peculiar and insolent young ladies.

"Not yet." She enunciated those two words as if she sought to educate a lackwit. "That is, however, why I'm suggesting we speak alone."

They engaged in a silent battle, stares locked, feet fixed to the floor.

Connell would be damned if he ceded this match.

Relaxing the forced-at-best smile she'd worn for the past two minutes, the young lady let loose a long sigh. "Very well."

Some of the tension left his shoulders. Splendid. She was...

Marching over to the baroque gilded sofa, Lady Constance gripped the ornately curved arms and set to work dragging it across the floor.

"My God, what in blazes are you doing?" he asked over the loud squeal of that furniture rearrangement.

"We can speak h-here if that is your wish," she panted from her exertions.

"I assure you, this is certainly *not* my wish," he called out as the sofa's legs scraped loudly over the marble. "In fact, if I had one hundred granted me, your remaining here would not come remotely close to so much as the last item upon it."

He might as well have been speaking to himself.

Grunting, the young woman dropped the sizable hall bench, and then undeterred, she planted her hip against it and proceeded to shove, before alternating her efforts back to carrying the baroque sofa.

Oh, Good God, this was really enough. "My offices, Lady Constance."

The young woman dropped the heavy-looking piece of furniture so that it sat in the middle of the foyer and gave it a contemplative glance. "Should I return it to its proper—"

"Now, Lady Constance," he snapped, already starting from the foyer, down the hall, and onward to his recently acquired Mayfair offices.

It'd been more than ten years since he'd broken it off with Lady Emilia, but the time had come at last. She was determined to have revenge upon him and had sent her vexing friend.

Connell quickened his steps.

But then, if that were true, Lady Emilia would have to care. Which she did not. She'd gone and married Connell's best friend, Heath, and upon Connell's last meeting with the young woman, she'd been anything but affected by Connell's presence. Therefore, revenge hardly fit, but how else to account for Lady Constance?

"Would you slow your strides?" Lady Constance said, puffing as she sought to keep up with him. "You're practically running."

Had he been a gentleman, he would have slowed his strides.

Alas, breaking off a betrothal years ago and now living the life of a recluse, hardly marked one any manner of a respectable sort.

"I'm not practically running," he said, not so much as deigning a look back at her.

"Very well, then you are running."

"That's the first thing you've gotten right this day," he muttered.

"What was that?" she called loudly, her voice carrying over the great distance he'd put between them. "I cannot hear you as far as you are."

Oh, bloody hell.

Connell stopped and spared a look at his stealer-of-peace.

The young woman, her skirts hiked up, was nearly upon him. With those skirts high as they were, she flashed a tantalizing view of… He hooded his eyes. *Naked ankles.* Naked ankles in the dead of winter, no less. That hint of cream-white flesh was delectably enticing.

Nay, he was no gentleman indeed.

"That is better," she said under her breath, wholly unaware he'd just been ogling her. For there could be no doubting that if she had, she'd have promptly run off in the opposite direction. "Sprinting about and leaving your company in the lurch." She let her skirts fall, stealing that tantalizing view and the only welcome part of her presence this day.

He didn't blink for several moments. "Are you… speaking about me?" As if he weren't even here.

The tart-minx gave an insolent flip of her curls. "If you're offended, I'd take a hard look at how you're behaving."

Iris had possessed governesses and nursemaids who could have learned a lesson or two on sternness from this one.

A memory of the little girl and her bright, mischievous smile slid forward.

He thinned his eyes into razor slits and took a step toward Constance Brandley. "Let us be clear, madam. 'Company' implies one who is invited, one who is welcome."

Of course the chit didn't back away. She angled her chin up in a like, defiant fury, and his annoyance only burned hotter.

"You, in fact, are neither. Not for me. And…" He flicked an icy stare over her. "I suspect not for anybody."

She gasped.

He continued over that indignant outrage. "Furthermore, if you are very interested in exchanging lessons on propriety and manners, let *your* first one be to advise you against visiting bachelor gentlemen."

There was a beat of silence.

"All bachelors."

He puzzled his brow.

"It's just, you said you'd advise me against paying visits to bachelor gentlemen."

As she prattled, he searched for—and failed to find—any indication that she jested.

"When in actuality, a woman concerned with propriety should steer clear of not just gentlemen bachelors, but *all* bachelors." The termagant worked her gaze up and down his person. "Your inability to acknowledge those men outside the peerage is no doubt a product of your ducal status. Of course," she tacked on.

Of course. Connell's brows lowered.

"In my offices, Lady Constance," he snapped. Turning on his heel, he started on the path forward to his rooms. This time at a modified pace.

Pushing her garish feathered bonnet back, the lady walked at his side, her clever gaze darting all around, taking in the arched ceiling with its gold latticework and the enormous pendant pair of still-life paintings, those nauseating gilded frames filled with vibrant blooms. Not a space had been spared upon the gold-painted walls, each inch covered in those oils on canvases.

Lady Constance's face pulled.

"Is there a problem, Lady Constance?" he drawled.

"It is… a bit much."

Much like his newly inherited insolent servants, the young lady didn't fawn or feed him niceties. And damned if he didn't find himself with an unexpected stirring of appreciation for the chit.

His afternoon guest paused beside a dusty golden oak hall table and examined the campana-shaped urn stuffed to overflowing with pink and red flowers so dusty they bore a coating of white. "Ah-ah—*choo.*" The young woman sneezed into her elbow.

He fished for a kerchief before registering his missing jacket.

Lady Constance shook her head. "In fact, it is not what I would have expected of your tastes, Your Grace."

Did she refer to the dust or the décor? Either way? Nothing about this address was his household. Not really. It had all been left by another, which was why he was here in the first place.

She gave him a curious look. "Nor was I aware you'd moved residences."

Connell dropped a hip on the side of the hall table. "You paid such close attention to my London address?"

She gave him an arch look. "Well, given the fact I thought my best friend would be living with you, yes, yes, I did."

Touché. His cheeks went hot.

He was blushing. Him. Not the young lady he'd intended to unnerve. Hurriedly straightening, Connell urged her on. "Let's go."

Not another word passed between them the whole rest of the way.

The moment they reached his offices, Connell shoved the door shut with the bottom of his boot. "Don't expect this to be a lengthy…"

The minx was already unfastening her cloak. Divesting herself of the pale green article, she draped it over the back of the leather button sofa and then glanced down at his jacket resting there.

"Meeting," he muttered. "What do you want?"

Picking up the dark wool garment, she held it over. "Might I suggest you don your jacket, Your Grace?"

"And is this so very relevant to your being here?" he drawled. And yet, he still grabbed it from her fingers and stuffed his arms into the article. In a childlike show of disobedience, however, he left the buttons undone.

"It's simply less distracting speaking to you when you're fully attired." The lady widened her eyes. "Er…"

Interesting.

For the first time since Iris and her mother had left, he found himself… smiling. More so, grinning. And by the suspicious glint in the lady's eyes, his was more the wolfish sort. Either way, he was… smiling.

Unnerved, he started for the marble-top sideboard laden with silver trays laden with crystal decanters. Grabbing the one nearest his fingertips, he also plucked up a glass and headed to his—*the* desk.

The lady eyed him with something akin to horror.

"Ah, forgive me," he said, his expression deadpan. Heading back to the stacked drink cart, he helped himself to another snifter and carried his bounty back. Adding several fingers of brandy into each glass, he held one out.

She gave it a long look, and then sweeping over, she accepted the glass. "Thank you."

Connell jerked his hand so quick, amber droplets spilled over the rim, splashing his fingers.

With a knowing and all-too-pleased little smile, Lady Constance took the drink, seated herself opposite him, and proceeded to take a measured swallow.

One that sent the long column of her throat working, and all at once, he noted two things. One, drinking spirits wasn't at all unfamiliar to the lady. And two, the arch of her neck as she drank was damnably erotic.

A detail he shouldn't be noting—not because he was a gentleman. He wasn't. But because she was the best friend of his former betrothed. And even that was a line he'd not cross.

The lady lowered her glass, yanking Connell's attention swiftly up and away from her. Studiously avoiding her gaze, he grabbed the sides of his chair, dragging it closer to the desk, and sat. When he at last made himself look at her, she'd already set aside her snifter for the bag she carried.

"Now," she began, all business. "I've come to help."

"I wasn't aware I was in need of help," he drawled.

"Oh, yes."

"Don't paint this as though it is for me," he snapped.

"Very well. It is for me. I run an advice column."

"An advice column?" he echoed loudly.

Clearing her throat, the lady glanced pointedly at the door.

She needn't bother with worries of passing servants. There were but two, and they were already snoring soundly after a morning spent drinking. Even if they had been awake, they wouldn't know whether the king himself had come to call and declared war upon France.

"I should clarify it is not necessarily mine. I've taken it over."

"You do show a remarkable talent for taking over," he muttered.

She beamed like he'd plucked the sun from summer and hung it outside the dreary, winter London-landscape.

"I wasn't complimenting you."

"Not intentionally, which makes it all the more appreciated. Therefore, I will thank you for the compliment."

He rubbed the sides of his temples. She and her confounded logic were giving him a damned megrim. "So, you've stolen an advice column."

That managed to kill her smile, and he was struck by the inextricable urge to call back his words, as her smile had been a hint of cheer when he'd been so bloody miserable and hadn't thought to again know any manner of lightness.

"I didn't steal it," she said crisply. She gave a little shake of her head, sending limp curls bouncing sadly about her shoulders. "I borrowed it."

"Borrowed it," he repeated.

It wasn't a question, but the lady nodded anyway.

"You don't *borrow* a column, madam."

"Anything can be lent and shared. Credit. Horses. Slippers. Gowns. Boots." When she paused to breathe, Connell opened his mouth, but the chit proceeded on with her enumeration. "Pencils. Dresses."

"You've said that one twice," he pointed out.

She tipped her head. "Did I?"

"You did."

"Hmph. Well, *trousers*, then."

He shot his brows up. "What blasted man would share trousers with other men?"

"I wasn't referring to men," she said, her features completely placid.

Her meaning registered, and his intrigue was piqued once more. And more, an image slipped in of the curvy Lady Constance stripped of a gown and clad in tight-fitting breeches that only further showed off those entrancing trim ankles.

Desire stirred.

"Though, I suspect," the young woman prattled casually on, effectively throwing water on that all-too-improper lust, "it's rather obsequious to expect that a man couldn't, or rather, *wouldn't* share his garments with others in need." She gave him a deliberate and judgmental look.

Desire?

Intrigue?

What in blazes had he been thinking?

Connell shook his head, hard. Good God, the world had been turned upside down. He was debating inanities that mattered not at all to him—or really, in the scheme of life—and lusting after his former betrothed's friend... a friend whom he'd little recollection of.

Funny, that. The charming, affable man he'd been of his youth would have appreciated this minx and her spirit.

She stared at him.

Something was expected of him here. An answer, no doubt.

"You want me to write your column."

She scoffed. "Hardly. I know little of your writing, but what I do recall left much to be desired." Her cheeks pinkened. "No offense intended," she added with a surprising contriteness.

Except...

Connell narrowed his eyes. "You read the notes I wrote to Lady Emilia."

"Were there notes? I only read the poems."

Another blaze of heat splotched his cheeks. Nay, it began at his neck and worked its way up his face. And never more had he, who abhorred the restraints of a cravat, wished to be wearing one to conceal the hint of his second blush that day. Connell dusted a hand over his face. "Yes, well, my poetry days ended long, long ago." Was there to be no end to his suffering? "I've not penned one in nearly ten years—"

"If I may continue?"

"Please," he said in flat tones that no one would ever dare construe as a true invitation.

Except, apparently, this woman.

"Thank you." She beamed. Her smile highlighted two deep dimples set amidst plump cheeks. Her eyes sparkled, and in a remarkably jolting realization, he saw that that pleased grin made an ordinary young miss... quite memorable. "Er... where was I?"

Connell really had no idea. "You wanted me to write your column?"

She sighed. "No. I don't want you to—" The lady froze midsentence and gave him a wide-eyed look. "You're teasing."

Connell started. Teasing? He'd not teased in six months now. Not since Iris' departure. "I was not," he said gruffly. It was simply something he didn't do anymore. The same as laugh and smile. The latter of which he'd now done twice since Lady Constance had shown up on his doorstep. "Will you just get on with it?"

"As you wish," she murmured, her knowing tones indicating she found him to be a liar. "I require your... input."

Somewhere in the far corners of his mind, a bell went off, ringing a warning. Of course, that could have also been a product of too much drink. "Of all the people whose input you might have sought out, you chose… *me?*"

"I did."

The scandalous scoundrel who'd jilted her best friend? The lady was off her head.

And mayhap he was as much dicked in the knob, for he should send her on her way, but instead, he found himself asking, "And just how might I help you?"

Her smile widened once more. "Splendid."

And then the third miracle of the day came. Connell laughed. It was a sharp bark, rusty and ragged from ill use, but real and driven by… hilarity. She thought… She believed he was… Connell laughed all the more.

The lady eyed him like he'd made his final descent into madness.

"I wasn't offering," he said when he'd gotten control of his amusement.

Her expression fell, and where there'd been a momentary flash of light in his otherwise miserable world, the slip of her smile ushered in more of the dark. It was a silly thought. One that made no sense. But then, nothing in Lady Constance's being here rang with any real logic or reason.

As quick as her dispiritedness had come, it left. A pleased smile back in place, Lady Constance lifted a triumphant finger. "But neither have you rejected my offer."

"Nay." He would, though. For now, however, he was enjoying himself. Connell kicked back on the hind legs of his chair. "Now, why don't you tell me—"

"I'd like your assistance in identifying five ways a lady might earn the heart of a duke."

CHAPTER 4

IT TOOK A MOMENT FOR Constance to register that she was speaking to empty air.

Of all the responses she might have expected from the Duke of Renaud, being knocked on his arse in surprise had not been one of them. Though, it was just as likely shock… or horror.

Constance exploded to her feet, and rushing around the desk, she peered down at the Duke of Renaud's prone form. "Oh, goodness."

He scowled up at her. "You're off your head."

Ignoring that curt utterance, she dropped to a knee. "Given that you are on your buttocks, you aren't doing very much better," she felt inclined to point out. And then the second wonder of wonders that day—the Duke of Renaud blushed. "Are you hurt?"

"Get out."

"I shall take that as a 'no,' then."

"Take it however you wish, my lady. Discussing the ways to… to…"

"Win your heart?"

He winced. "*That*," he muttered, "is not something I intend to speak with you on."

"Because you're Emilia's former betrothed?"

The color on his cheeks deepened. "Because I don't have a heart," he snapped.

"Yes. Well, I won't disagree with you there," she said under her breath.

His brows came flying together. "What was that?"

"I said we can't leave you lying there," she glibly supplanted, and his ever-narrowing gaze called Constance out as a liar.

Odd, her oldest and earliest remembrances of the Duke of Renaud were of a carefree rogue. She'd not, however, taken him as the clever sort.

More the fool she.

"Get out," he said for a second time.

In fairness, he'd entertained Constance far longer than she'd anticipated and far longer than any other gentleman would have.

It didn't fit with the way that she viewed him—as a self-absorbed scoundrel.

Oh, he was still a bounder. He'd always be one. But he'd been patient and willing to hear her out, which was more than she'd expected. "Either way…" She carried on as if he'd not just ordered her gone for now a second time. "If it is any manner of consolation, I'm not trying to teach women how to win *your* heart."

"That is hardly a consolation." Bypassing Constance's outstretched fingers, the duke pushed up onto his elbows and, with an impressive agility, leaped to his feet so that Constance was left kneeling where he'd last lain.

"Because… because…" All words left her. For it was hard not to be even a little awed by the ease of that athleticism. Particularly given that most lords wore padding to present a façade of manliness. Despite herself, despite good judgment and loyalty to Emilia, Constance couldn't resist stealing a peek at the bulges of his biceps… and triceps and… blast, the whole of his arms. Her belly fluttered dangerously, and she briefly closed her eyes in a bid to regain control of her addled senses.

"Because?" he prodded.

Because…?

What was he saying? Nay, what had she been saying? Everything was all scrambled in her head.

"Are we certain you aren't the one that hit your head?" he drawled when Constance still hadn't found her voice.

She opened her eyes, and the lord was mocking her. Or calling her out for being the disloyal friend she was for staring at the well-defined, sculptor-carved limbs before her.

"I can't much be certain of anything," she muttered, hating the breathless quality of the utterance she'd intended as droll. She made herself place her palm in his, allowing him to pull her to her feet, praying he didn't notice the slight tremble to her fingers.

Tremble?

What in thunderation moment of madness was this? She was Constance Brandley, confirmed spinster, loyal friend to Emilia Aberdeen, now Whitworth, advice columnist. Granted, a rather unsuccessful advice columnist. That managed to bring her back to her purpose here.

"I'm not necessarily looking to teach ladies how to win your heart, but rather, the hearts of... other dukes."

He strangled on something that might have been a laugh. "And there are so many unmarried dukes in England that you're writing an entire column on it?" Except, as he spoke, his face remained impassive.

"Are you laughing at me, Your Grace?"

"Do you take me as one given to fits of hilarity?"

Constance peered at his classically beautiful, sharp features that were set in a perfect mask and the hard lines of his mouth. "No," she allowed. "You don't. You look altogether different than..." She clamped her lips shut to keep from finishing the thought and studiously avoided his eyes. She looked about his office, at the pair of unlikely Meissen porcelain urns, to the nearly iridescent girandole sconces with mirrors. At anything except him.

Alas, he'd not be so gentlemanly as to allow her that retreat.

"Different than what, Lady Constance?"

Constance reluctantly forced her attention over. Her skin prickled from the heat of the gaze he trained on her.

He folded his arms at his broad chest. Had he always been so broad? A triangle of golden curls peeked from the top of—

"From my *younger* self?"

Face flaming, she whipped her eyes up to his. "Scowling," she blurted. It was the first time in the whole of her life that she'd ever seen that hint of a man's chest. That was, a real-life breathing man and not the ones she'd spied on canvas. She fought the desperate urge to fan herself. "Surly, and sarcastic, and—"

"Are there any other S words you intend to level at me?" he drawled.

Sexy. She choked. "Sour. You're not at all as I remember you." Rather, he fit with the solitary figure his former ward had described in her sad little note. For the first time since Constance had arrived, she felt a stirring of pity for the gentleman.

Something traipsed across his features, a glimmer of sadness that sparked in his eyes, and she wanted to call the words back, preferring him sarcastic and surly to... this. But then he flashed a small, wolfish grin that accentuated the pearl white of his even teeth. "You remember me, then."

Constance rolled her eyes. "Still arrogant as ever, I see."

With that, they were restored to a more even ground.

"Before we begin with a rundown of words starting with A, might I issue a word of advice?"

She nodded. "You ma—"

"Don't go matching ladies looking to you for marital advice with men who are surly, sour, sarcastic, and arrogant."

It was actually rather good advice.

"What made you come to me?" He righted his chair. "Of all gentlemen, you chose..." Emilia's former betrothed. That remained between them, and as long as she secured his assistance, that relationship would *stay* between them.

"I..." Something, however, kept her from mentioning his young ward. Something that had everything to do with the sadness that surrounded him. No man as proud as the Duke of Renaud would take to knowing a child had intervened on his behalf. "I... Most of respectable Society is gone for the winter." There, that much was true.

"Don't you have a brother?"

His words brought Constance forward on the balls of her feet. "You know Hadden?"

"We've never moved in the same circles."

That small, fledgling hope died. "Oh. Of course." She should have known that. She'd never known much about her younger brother and had been left with only more questions about the sibling who spent his years abroad. Feeling the duke's eyes on her, she cleared her throat. "I don't... He..." Her chest tightened. "I don't know where he is. My family doesn't," she said softly. It was a detail the *ton* didn't know, and yet, she'd gone and shared it with this man.

It's only because you require his assistance, too, and as such, it was only fair to be candid where she could. Liar.

Constance twisted her fingers in the fabric of her dress before catching his gaze on the distracted movement. She made herself stop. "Nor was I the manner of sister who was ever really friendly or familiar with his friends." Hadden had kept to his friends, and Constance had had the bonds of Emilia, Aldora, Meredith, and Rowena. And all the years since her younger and only sibling had been gone, she'd mourned never having taken time to know him. "As such, I'm rather... limited in my options."

She caught a wry flash of amusement.

"And you are a duke. Therefore, given the question I've received, it makes altogether sense that you would be the one I might seek out for... help."

And in that, they might help each other.

He stared at her for a long while, revealing nothing, saying even less.

The pretty ormolu clock atop his white-painted mantel ticked away the time.

He hadn't said no... *yet*. But he would. Why, the way he studied her even now, he merely toyed with her. Toyed with her as he had since she'd entered. And when he rejected her outright? Then where would she be... and where would he be? She'd not help him as his previous ward had implored.

Finally, he spoke. "What would this"—he unfurled his arms and slashed a hand between them—"entail?"

Hope lent her heart an extra beat in its rhythm. He was actually thinking about it? "I... It wouldn't require much, really."

He snorted. "Not requiring much means you're not darkening my doorstep, and yet, here we are."

Yes, here they were indeed. "I'm providing young ladies with guidance on—"

"How to win the title of duchess?"

Her lips tugged down at the corners, but she refused to rise to his bait. "However, the column is really just general information as to how a lady might…" Entrance a duke. Ensnare a duke. Either way, any way, she couched it, was His Grace really all that wrong on what her column was or would be? Shoving back that discomfiting detail, she cleared her throat. "How a lady might stand out above the rest," she settled for.

Folding his arms once more, he drummed his fingertips along his lawn sleeves. "How much time would you require?"

Constance looked around, lingering her gaze on the pipe resting on the floor beside a brightly painted vase and a bottle of brandy. "Are you otherwise too busy?"

He followed her stare and looked back. "I'm fairly certain you're the only woman stupid enough to insult the very person she's seeking a favor from," he said dryly. There was a ghost of a smile on his hard lips.

Her pulse jumped.

Surely she imagined that tilt of his mouth? Or the dizzying effect it had on her senses?

And mayhap this was how Emilia had committed the greatest folly in falling for him.

Thrusting back that madness, she refocused on her entire purpose in being here. "I won't require more than a week of your time."

"Too much."

"Six—"

"Nope."

She stamped her foot. He was toying with her. That was all there was to it. "Why don't you tell me what *you're* willing—"

"Five days."

Hmph. "Well, that seems rather arbitrary, Your Grace."

"Are you familiar with the numerology of the number five?"

She blinked slowly. "I… uh… No."

"The number five generally indicates a person who is full of energy and yet unable to channel it responsibly. That is you."

Well. She'd be offended if she weren't so riveted by his understanding of… "Numerology, you say?" she murmured. "Perhaps… you should be the one writing the column, after all,

Your Grace." Her words weren't said in jest or mockery, but rather, born of a fascination with his… knowledge.

"You have five days," he fired back. "I don't rise early, so see that you're punctual."

It took a moment for the meaning to sink in. "You expect me to come here?" she blurted. "To your *townhouse*." She couldn't very well go about bringing cheer to his life by simply sitting here, taking notes on anything and everything he was willing to share.

He looked around his office. "I'm confused. Isn't that where we are meeting now?"

Her mind raced. "Of course it is," she said simply, and when he only continued to stare at her in abject confusion, Constance let out an exaggerated sigh. She went on to explain. "It was no small risk in coming here."

"You also pointed out London is largely empty of the proper company."

"Yes, but sneaking out but once to journey here is one matter. To do so for five days…" She shuddered. "I'd be dancing with ruin." Constance gave him a long look. "We'd both be dancing with ruin." There, that should bring him 'round. The last thing a scoundrel wished for was to be caught in a compromising position with a lady.

He closed his eyes, and his lips moved as if he were praying. When he opened his eyes, he wore his all-too-familiar annoyance in every chiseled plane of his face. "And we'd be eminently safer meeting *in public*?"

She puzzled her brow. Well, when he said it that way…

"You didn't think this part through."

She shook her head. "I… I'm afraid I did not." Constance proceeded to pace before his gleaming mahogany desk. She couldn't come here every day. Not, as she'd pointed out, without risking ruin and discovery. *Or is it simply that you worry about being alone here, in his residence, with the world none the wiser of your meetings?*

Constance stopped abruptly. "Chance meetings."

"I'm not following," he said flatly.

She gestured wildly as she spoke. "You're asking for my help and expecting that I join you… at the Royal Museum and public libraries and Hatchards bookshop?"

She smiled, feeling rather pleased—

"That is a daft idea."

Her smile slipped. The curmudgeon. Constance bristled, forgetting for a moment the very reason she sought to convince him and focusing instead on that insult. "It's a perfectly reasonable one, Your Grace."

He chuckled. "There's been nothing reasonable about your entire visit here."

He'd another point there.

Looping his twined fingers behind his head, he resumed his study of her, and she resisted the urge to shift under that focus. "You wish for my cooperation? Then my rules. My townhouse. You can have your five days with a duke, Constance. And not a day more." Letting his arms drop to the desk, he held his palm out across the immaculate surface.

She worried at her lower lip. Seated as he was, like a golden-haired devil upon his throne, he bartered the way Lucifer might with mere mortals foolish enough to tangle with him. "Very well." Before she thought better of it, and opted for a safer route for her article, and abandoned the little girl who'd solicited Constance's help, she placed her fingers in Connell's.

A shock of heat scorched through the flimsy fabric of her worn leather gloves and sent a trail of dangerous tingles radiating from her wrist up the whole length of her arm. Constance yanked her fingers back. "I–it is settled, Your Grace," she stammered. The reed-thin quality of her voice played off his high ceilings, putting her unease on embarrassing display. Hurrying to gather up her bag, she stuffed her belongings into it and dropped a hasty curtsy. Constance made for the door.

She didn't make it any more than five steps.

"Oh, and Constance?" he called, stopping her in her tracks.

Not, however, because of his command. Rather, because... of her name.

Constance. She'd long viewed it as a grand-mère's name. Perfectly suited to an old, unmarried spinster, which was precisely what she was.

And yet, as those normally harsh syllables rolled from this man's tongue, they slid forth like a silken caress. She paused, dread bringing her slowly back, a fear that had nothing to do with the possibility he'd had second thoughts about their arrangement and everything to do with her body's physical awareness of him. "Yes, Your Grace?"

"Christian names," he murmured, strolling closer with sleek pantherlike steps that continued to wreak havoc on her heart's natural beat. The duke... *Connell*, stopped with just a pace between them. "Given we've five days alone together, we'll dispense with formalities."

The notorious Duke of Renaud uttering her name in his wickedly deep, honeyed baritone? Day in and day out for five days? "B-but..."

"Christian names, Constance," he purred, possessing her name as though it was his, and in that moment, she would have gladly given it to him for nothing more than an assurance that he'd say it over and over.

Constance stumbled back a step, tripping over the hem of her dress and cloak in her bid to get away... or to break this magnetic pull. "V-very well, Y-Your—Connell." And with that, she collected her skirts and fled.

"Until tomorrow," he called.

There was a good deal more wickedness in her soul than she'd credited, for as Constance made her escape, she found herself eager for their first day together.

CHAPTER 5

THE FOLLOWING MORNING, CONNELL, STATIONED at the floor-length windows of the garish front parlor, puffed away upon his newly inherited pipe. Around the cloud of smoke left by the little ivory instrument, he peered down at the quiet streets below.

Just as he'd been peering for the better part of two hours.

Not that he was eager for Constance Brandley's company. Not at all.

She was… simply a diversion. Nothing more. This anticipation was really just a product of his boredom, one that suggested he'd be wise to seek out the old haunts and past pleasures he'd once found in London.

So why did the idea of endless nights drinking and carousing at his wicked clubs not stir the same eagerness as the prospect of sparring with the tart-mouthed, feisty minx?

Connell took another slow puff.

They should have settled on a time. After all, she'd left him waiting around all day.

Not that he'd otherwise had plans this day… or any day, which had been an idleness he'd preferred.

That, however, had been before his unlikeliest of afternoon visitors.

He straightened, his gaze catching on a distant fleck of a figure on the horizon. That same pea-green cloak, which stood out stark and bright amidst the dreary gray London landscape, wasn't in the manner of color that would spare her notice.

In fact, it was a hue and quality better suited to an older matron than the full-cheeked, bright-eyed beauty who'd come here yesterday.

She drew nearer, walking with a brisk, determined clip, and he caught sight of his visage reflected back. The small grin had come naturally, when he'd not found a reason to smile since…

Just like that, the brief interlude he'd found this day vanished, replaced with a reminder of his losses. And his new life. One that was so very empty, he found himself hovering about, awaiting the company of a damned lady—a lady who was also his former betrothed's best friend. And who was coming 'round only because she required assistance with an advice column.

Now the crystal pane reflected back Connell's scowl. At that very moment, the lady stopped below, tilted her head back, and found him. She returned his frown.

Even with the fifty feet of distance that divided them, he caught the way she wrinkled her pert nose before sweeping up the steps and reaching for the knocker.

She let that gold lion fall once. Twice. And then stopped.

With an inexplicable spring to his step, Connell made the trek to the foyer.

Through the gossamer curtains over the window, he caught her standing there, rubbing her gloved fingers together. He hastened his strides and drew the door open.

Not missing a beat, Constance swept inside, and he pushed the panel shut behind them. "You really do not have servants, do you?" she asked, her voice carrying around the soaring foyer.

"I'm a duke," he drawled. "Do you truly believe I don't have servants?" It wasn't altogether a lie. He'd two of them. That surely counted.

From under her big bonnet, she looked at him with bemused eyes. "Have you hidden them all away?"

"In a way," he muttered. The pair had hidden themselves away. Jennie and James were now on their second nap of the day. Curiosity piqued in the young lady's features, and Connell shook his head. "Don't ask."

He needn't have worried. Dropping her bag at her feet, Constance had already dismissed him. Unclasping the grommet of her heinous pea-green muslin cloak, she removed the article and…

Connell choked a bit on his swallow.

The lady's bustle silk dress, adorned with ribbons and bows and lace and… well, every other damned adornment that might be affixed to a gown, might as well have been pulled from the last century. Green silk brocade shoes with straps for buckles peeked out from under the hemline. And yet, garish as the dress was, the raised, fitted waistline brought all focus to the low neck that put her voluptuous bosom on display.

Connell's mouth went dry as a wave of lust bolted through him, and in a bid to control something, anything, he took another puff from his pipe.

The lady gave a toss of her impressive curls, sending a sad feather flopping over her eyes. "Do you have a problem with my attire, Your Grace?" she asked, shoving that puce monstrosity back into place.

His ears going hot, Connell whipped his gaze up to her affronted one. "I have a greater problem with your still Your Gracing me." Although, he'd an equal problem with his absolute fixation on her beautiful bosoms.

"I'm something of an eccentric." The lady adjusted her feather adornment, her fingers toying with her voluminous golden curls and stirring up more of that unwanted appreciation and awareness of the proper miss. "I prefer *classic* clothing."

And by *classic*, the lady meant garments in vogue when she was in the cradle. He exhaled a cloud of smoke. "I… see that," he said through the little cloud of white. And Connell rather found himself with a preference for her out-of-mode choice of dress. Or, more specifically, her in it.

Her thick lashes swept low, and her annoyance spilled through the pinpricks of her eyes.

She'd mistaken his words and study of her as unfavorable, and the gentleman he'd been long ago would have disabused her of that affront. He'd have pointed out that it was a wicked rogue's desire and appreciation for her lush form that earned his focus. "Shall we?" he said instead, holding an arm out.

With another little flounce of her curls, she started forward with a purposeful step so that he was left staring after her, at the V formed by the fabric that gave a nice little point down to the lady's buttocks. As if further attention needed to be drawn to that well-rounded flesh, four buttons had been sewn into a little square, framing that delectable sight. Each sideways sway of her hips as she walked was a further enticement. One that tempted. Taunted.

With his spare hand, Connell loosened his cravat.

Constance tossed a glance over her shoulder, and it jolted him into movement. Jolted him into thinking of anything other than the sight or sway of her generously curved hips.

It had been too long since he'd had a woman. That was all there was to it.

He was in London. A lover would rectify this inexplicable lust for a lady who dressed like a woman from bygone times. A proper spinster at that, working on an advice column. Yes, he'd see to that. Not her column, but a woman to fix in his bed. A warm, willing, eager widow.

One who didn't scowl and wrinkle her nose as the lady laying command of his halls.

So why would his mind not focus on the thought of anyone but the tart-mouthed little general who'd somehow gotten him to agree to five daily visits?

Unnerved and eager to get this day started and then over with, he gave silent thanks when they reached his offices. Her little satchel swinging as she went, Constance marched the length of the room. "After you," he said dryly, sweeping an arm out toward the seat she'd already claimed opposite his desk. He shut the door behind them.

Head bent, she proceeded to rummage around in her sizable bag, the leather mail satchel as odd a choice as the lady's dress, or the woman herself.

As Connell took up the place beside her, the lady paused in her searching and turned a frown up at him. "What are you doing?" she blurted.

Connell took another slow puff of his pipe. "I think it should be fairly clear." He stretched his legs out and crossed them at the ankles. "I'm sitting."

That adorable frown puckered the place between her eyebrows. "Yes, I can *seeee* that," she said, managing to add two extra beats to that word. "I mean, what are you doing... there?" She waved a pencil in his general direction.

"And where *should* I be seated?"

Constance jabbed the writing utensil as sorry as her feather at the other side of the desk.

Connell followed her gesture. He opened his mouth, but called back the droll response as an understanding dawned. Why, not unlike his unnerving response to her, the indomitable minx wasn't immune to him, either. He set his pipe on the arm of his chair. Well, this was interesting. Finding a renewed enjoyment with this unlikely arrangement, Connell crossed his arms and rested them behind his head. "Just why do you expect I should sit... there?"

"I..." Her cheeks pinkened. "Why don't we just begin, then?" she countered instead, digging around her peculiar bag once more. Constance withdrew an old leather notebook, flipped through page after page filled with a sloppy childlike scrawl.

Making a show of gathering his pipe, he squinted at her recordings.

As if feeling his stare on her work, the lady whipped her head up. She turned another frown on him before angling the aged book closer to herself and away from his scrutiny. "Why don't we begin with what manner of pleasures you enjoy?"

Connell promptly dissolved into a paroxysm.

And yet, there had been nothing suggestive in her tone or in her expressive eyes. In fact, those eyes revealed nothing less than annoyance.

"Are you choking on that horrific smoke? Or have I said something to amuse you?"

"Th-the latter," he said when he'd regained the ability to draw proper breath.

By the slight parting of her full lips, that frankness had not been what Constance had been expecting.

Connell abandoned his relaxed repose, and sitting up, he leaned closer to her. "Do you really wish to know the manner of...

pleasures I enjoy?"

Her mouth formed a perfect circle as wide as her rounded eyes as his meaning set in.

"You are still a scoundrel," she muttered, and Connell found himself grinning as she scribbled something in her little book. He would have traded his soul to know just what she'd written there.

"Ah, love, but I never presumed to be anything but," he purred.

The color deepened on her cheeks, a delectable bright blush that should have annoyed him because of its innocence. And yet, he was only further enticed.

"How do you prefer to spend your time? That is, other than smoking on a pipe, as all old dukes do?"

He blinked slowly. "*Old* dukes?"

"Squinting. Smoking on a pipe. Surly and snarly." As she spoke, she directed every last charge not at Connell but at her musty little book. "And given your faltering hearing, I'm fairly certain you've met all the requisites for proper ducal behavior."

And here one would believe that quick-fire cataloging couldn't be more insulting.

"I assure you, my hearing isn't faltering," he clipped out.

From under her breath, she said something that sounded very like, "That can certainly be debated."

Connell straightened in his chair. "What was that?" he barked.

She lifted her head once more, this time to flash a triumphant smile. "Precisely my point."

Connell's eyebrows shot up. The damned imp.

"Continuing on," she said. "You were sharing your pleas— pastimes."

Pastimes.

His gaze slid over to the heavy gold curtains, drawn neatly back and tied, letting in the bright afternoon sun.

How very different that answer would have been to the man he'd once been. Riding, carousing, drinking, wagering. A dissolute lifestyle was the only existence he'd known until he'd met Emilia. And then after Emilia? More specifically, after he'd *ended it with* Emilia, everything had changed. All his joys, his every pleasure, had centered around the pair he'd inherited.

His morns had been spent playing shuttlecock and battledore with a child whom no governess had managed to tame... and whom he'd not wished to see tamed.

His rides had been in the company of a little girl.

His card matches had been replaced with spillikins and other child's games.

"I trust there is... something you enjoy?" Constance ventured. Only, this query was stripped of the earlier sarcasm. And was all the worse for the gentleness that lined her question.

"Of course I enjoyed... things." Connell shifted on his seat, and the leather groaned, a tell marking him as the liar he was. For the truth was, he couldn't think of anything. His life had been so entwined with Iris and her mother that his identity and even the joy he'd taken had been fused with others.

"Enjoyed," Constance said in a quiet voice, pulling Connell's attention back to the woman responsible for this increasing disquiet.

He shook his head slowly. "I don't..."

Constance rested her book on her lap. Then, catching the underside of her chair, she dragged it around so they faced each other and then closer so their knees brushed. "You said 'enjoyed.' You spoke in the past tense."

Those words belonged to one who saw too much. Her piercing gaze saw even more and left him exposed before this woman who was indirectly linked to his past. "I didn't," he said coolly, setting his jaw. "I assure you there are many enjoyments I find."

She pursed her mouth. "Aside from your carnal pleasures."

Carnal pleasures.

It was hardly an illecebrous way to describe the act of lovemaking.

And yet, those two words dripping from *her* pursed mouth sent a heat through him.

"I never said 'carnal pleasures,' Constance," he reminded, walking his two middle fingers up her forearm, only the ancient fabric of her dress a thin, barely there barrier between them. With their legs touching as they were, he felt the tremble that worked through her body.

"V-very well. Th-then, what do you enjoy?"

Being with her. Sparring with her. He found an inexplicable and inordinate enjoyment in that, too. And aside from this unlikeliest of pleasures, there really was nothing. It was a pitiable, sorry truth he'd never dare admit to her. Or anyone. He searched his mind, considered her question, thought about who he'd once been and then leaned still closer. "Do you want to know what I enjoy, Constance?" he murmured.

She gave a shaky nod, and that feather adornment affixed to her hair bobbed its agreement.

"Dancing."

Their gazes locked. Her eyes lit, and then with a wide smile, she forgot him, and the only thing that mattered was her notebook. "Splendid. Do you have a favorite dance?"

A favorite dance?

He'd teased at seduction, so what accounted for the very real irritation that she'd so easily switched her focus over to quizzing him?

He shifted once more in his seat. "I do."

"And which set is it?" she returned as she scribbled.

What in hell…?

"Are you… *interviewing* me?"

She paused midwriting and finally looked at him again. "How else did you see this going, Conn—" Her words ended on a sharp gasp as he plucked the book from her fingers. "I beg your pardon." Fire flashed in her eyes, and it was a fluid shift from businesslike interviewer to feisty virago.

"You're forgiven," he muttered, reading the heading at the center of the page and the handful of sentences she'd recorded under it. He'd not really given too much thought before this moment to how their five days together would be spent. But he'd expected it to be deucedly more interesting than sitting like he was in sessions at Eton again. And all Connell knew was he preferred them teasing to… working.

"I'll have you know, I most certainly was *not* apologizing." She grabbed for her book.

Connell held it beyond her reach. "Mrs. Matcher's Guide to Landing the Heart of a Duke," he read aloud. He glanced up.

Abandoning her rescue attempts, the minx folded her hands primly on her lap and at least had the good grace to blush. "It's not *the* article," she said. A defensive note crept into her voice. "Not yet."

"No, it most certainly isn't." He resumed his reading.

Mrs. Matcher's Guide to Landing the Heart of a Duke. Rule one: It is essential to find out the gentleman's ~~pleasures~~ *interests.*

"You're not very good at this, are you?" he asked without inflection.

Even so, Constance bristled with indignation. "I beg your—?" The lady caught herself, stopping midsentence. She proceeded to tug off her leather gloves, the articles as old as the book in her lap. Then she set them on the arm of her chair.

She didn't speak for several moments, just smoothed her palms along the white petticoat displayed down the center of her dress. "And you know so very much about writing an advice column?" she asked evenly.

"I know that enumerating points isn't going to grab anyone's interest. I know that readers wish to be pulled in and then stay there on the pages of whatever you've written and…" He looked down. "Mrs. Matcher's Guide to Landing the Heart of a Duke. Rule one: It is essential to find out the gentleman's…" He held her gaze. "*Interests.*"

"Well, when you read it *that* way," she mumbled, slouching in her chair.

Another of those unexpected grins tugged at his lips. "I trust the advice you give is generally direct and straightforward?"

"Those mean the same thing," she muttered.

"And you're always this clinical," he spoke over her interruption. Connell stood.

Constance tipped her head back. "What are you doing?"

"We're done here."

"We're done?" Her face fell, and it was hard not to feel some lightness inside at that response. Even as that response was likely driven largely—or only—by the help she'd sought from him.

"In *here*," he clarified. "If we're going to speak on my fondness for dancing, we're going to have that discussion where it should be had."

Constance's throat worked slowly. "And… where is that, Connell?"

He grinned. "Why, the ballroom, of course."

CHAPTER 6

WHY, THE BALLROOM, OF COURSE.

Only, as Constance allowed herself to be escorted through the duke's palatial mansion, there was no *of course* about it.

It was scandalous and outrageous enough that she was here at all. But there was little need… Nay, there was no need to visit the ballroom with him.

Because she might be a virgin at thirty, but she was not so naïve as to think there wasn't some larger purpose of her joining him *in* that ballroom.

This wasn't supposed to be how the day went.

She was to have been in full control—of the questions, of the topics, of the meeting location. At no point had she thought he would take command of… all.

And she'd certainly not expected to find herself with him in a ballroom… alone.

Be it his ballroom or his offices, is it really all that different?

Despite that voice of reason echoing in her head, the logical part of her soul called her out as a liar.

For here, in the grand ballroom with its parquet floors and gilded frames and ivory paint, their exchange wasn't all business.

Just as she'd not expected this man to have formed such an accurate reading of her abilities as an advice columnist. He didn't know her. Not truly and not at all.

A gentleman who was, even with the shared connection they had to the past, ultimately a stranger, and yet from nothing more than the questions she'd put to him, he'd pinpointed precisely the struggles she was having as Mrs. Matcher.

The only consolation—and it was a small one at that—was they'd been searching his household for nearly twenty minutes now without successfully locating the room in question.

"How in blazes did they hide the damned ballroom?" Connell muttered as he tossed open another door.

To another parlor.

Pale pink and white and gold. Like the rest of the rooms, the parlor was filled to overflowing with fripperies and adornments that would have seen the Brandleys' comfortable for the remainder of their lives. With funds enough to pay for the cello she'd lost.

Connell pulled the door shut on that dream and started them back on their search.

"We don't really need to discuss this outside of your offices," she pointed out for the sixth time.

"You've said as much." He infused a droll edge into his tone. "Seven times."

She frowned. "It's only been six."

"The Pink Parlor One. Pink Parlor Two. The breakfast room. The dining room. The receiving room and Pink Parlor Six."

He paused in the middle of the corridor, eyeing a pair of double doors at the very end of the hall.

"That's still only six," she pointed out.

"And the billiards room," he added distractedly. That last item on his list, however, was spoken more to himself as he started quickly for the beautiful, intricately carved oak panels.

Hmph. Who'd have believed him so clever with those details?

Constance hastened after him. "Very well, six or seven times. That is neither here nor there. The simple matter is we're wasting time when—"

Connell pulled both doors open simultaneously, and Constance's breath hitched.

"We've found it," he said, as triumphant as one of those first conquerors to set out for the New World.

"Yes," she breathed. They had.

An ornate ceremonial staircase swept down into a gilded room. At the very opposite end of the hall, six curved window panels spanning the length of the fifty-foot ceilings allowed a generous dose of the sun's rays to stream in.

Eight floor-length crystal mirrors framed in gold hung on either side of the ballroom, casting the lavish space in an even brighter light. Ornate gold sconces dripping with crystals added to the glow of the room. So bright that not even a chandelier was required.

Constance arched her head back and stared overhead so long the muscles in her neck ached. A mural of *The Triumph of Apollo* had been painted in soft pastels suited to the color scheme of the rest of the elaborate townhouse. "It is magnificent," she whispered.

"It's a duplication." Pulling her attention away from the masterpiece, she glanced over at Connell. "There's nothing original in this household. They preferred their pinks and their golds and simply sought to re-create the grandest of the gold rooms."

Using his middle two fingers, he circled that painting she'd just been admiring. "It is *The Triumph of Apollo*. It is nothing more than a copy of Guido Reni. And the room," he went on, gesturing to the space below them, "is nothing more than a perfect likeness of the ballroom in Catherine Palace."

Just as she couldn't have ever predicted that the man she remembered from her youth should know how to begin her Mrs. Matcher's column so that she didn't bore young ladies to tears, he should also prove knowledgeable on paintings and décor. "You have an appreciation for art?" she blurted.

"I—" He grinned wryly. "You're ready for rule two?"

Rule two? Then his question registered, and the reason for his assumption, and her chest constricted from terror at knowing her question had had nothing to do with Mrs. Matcher. "No," she said quietly, even as lying was by far the safer option in this moment. "I was more… wondering." *About you.*

She curled her fingers hard around her old leather notebook.

"I'm no artist. I can't sketch worth a damn. But I enjoyed studying art." His expression grew wistful. "I'd traveled the Continent, and I always thought to do so again. I intended to," he added, caught in his own reminiscences.

Constance worked her gaze over the sharp, beautiful planes of his face. Every opinion she'd ever carried about Connell, the Duke of Renaud, had come from his relationship with Emilia. In that, he might as well have been a caricature of a person. He'd been a rogue. A scoundrel. And a lord bad at poetry. She'd not considered that he was a man with interests and passions. And certainly not for art. But then, what had she known of him then, and what did she really know of him now, to have based that assumption? How much else had she been wrong about where the gentleman was concerned? "Why did you stop?" she asked quietly. He'd funds enough to travel.

He shook his head as if rejoining her in the moment. "I met—"

Emilia.

His betrothal.

Constance's best friend.

It hung there, not needing to be spoken.

It was a much-needed reminder that this man whose services she'd engaged and whom she'd come to help at the behest of a young girl was, in fact, Emilia's former betrothed. And nothing that transpired between them over the next five days would ever matter more than those details.

Oddly, that left her… bereft. Which was silly. Why should she feel any way about the Duke of Renaud? There was only one purpose he served, and that was all that mattered.

And she felt like the biggest of liars that she couldn't even convince herself to believe that lie.

"Shall we?" he asked, jerking her back to the present. Connell held an elbow out, and she hesitated, knowing that placing her fingertips atop his sleeve would lend further mayhem to logic and reason.

He lifted a brow, and she was helpless.

Clutching her notebook and pencil in one hand, Constance allowed him to escort her down the carpeted stairway that widened with each step. The enormous room lent volume to their quiet footfalls, adding an echo as they walked.

They reached the bottom of the stairs, and he immediately released her, walking off as though she were an afterthought and continuing on to the center of the dance floor.

"Now, where were we?"

He'd taken her words and turned them on her. And what was worse? Constance didn't have a bloody clue as to what to ask or where they'd been prior to this moment. Fumbling with her book, she flipped through the pages. *Pleasures. Pastimes. The ballroom.* "Dancing," she blurted, reading the handful of sentences she'd recorded. And she felt the blush as it burned across her body. "Not together, that is," she said, her words tripping over one another. "We weren't dancing. We were speaking of dukes"—Amusement lit his eyes. That glimmer softened the cynical glint she'd spied there since their first meeting—"and their appreciation for… dancing," she finished lamely.

"I trust you wish to provide your ladies with advice on which sets as part of rule one?"

"They aren't *rules*, per se. They are…" She caught the grin on his lips and swatted his arm with her book. Flipping her childhood journal open, she found the place where she'd left off with her notes. "And I trust your favorite dance is…" Constance lowered her voice to an exaggerated husky whisper. "*The waltz.* For the opportunity it affords you to pull a lady close and clasp her waist and steal a forbidden touch." Except, in her bid to tease, her words conjured an image of her twined in Connell's strong arms.

"No, the waltz is not my top favorite," he said dryly. "Mayhap not even my second."

She eyed him dubiously. "Impossible."

"Because I'm a rogue?" As his was a rhetorical question, she saved herself from answering. "Though you presented a very worthy sale of that particular dance, no, it isn't." Connell winked.

Her cheeks warmed at that flutter of his golden lashes and from what she'd inadvertently revealed through her assumptions.

"And I assure you, Constance, I've not been a rogue in many years," he murmured.

What must he have been like when he'd been an unapologetic scoundrel? No lady would have stood a chance against his charm. And Emilia hadn't…

Hating that intrusion for reasons she didn't understand, Constance made a show of jotting some notes. "Very well. If not the waltz, what, then?"

Clasping his hands behind his back, he strolled closer, and with each step he took, her heart thudded a heavy, wild beat. He stopped a handbreadth away so their bodies nearly brushed, and as she tipped her head back to meet his gaze, her mouth went dry. "The mazur," he murmured.

She didn't blink for several moments, and then the spell was blessedly broken. A laugh exploded from her lips. "Th-the mazur. The *mmmmazur?*" she repeated before he had a chance to confirm that she'd heard him correctly.

He flicked her nose. "Tsk-tsk. Poor Constance. Judging the dance unfairly as you have, you've missed out all these years." He dangled that as a dare and an invitation as one.

And yet, he couldn't know that she'd missed out on dancing through no fault of her own. That the invitations for any set had ceased about six years ago, and even then, the only names to fill her card had been the desperate gentlemen who'd sought connections... and wealth. All the while, had they been in possession of the truth of her circumstances, they wouldn't have even offered that. "You're making light."

He scoffed. "Not at all." Connell held a hand out.

She balked. "What are you...?"

"What are *we* doing?" he finished for her. "We are dancing the mazurka."

He was mad. *This* was mad.

But then, perhaps *she* was mad, because Constance found herself dropping her things, placing her fingers in his, and following him to the middle of the ballroom floor.

Connell stopped so that they were positioned side by side, hand in hand.

They faced each other, and he sang. "ta TA TA ta TA TA."

Constance dipped a curtsy to his bow.

"ta TA TA ta TA TA," he continued to sing as they faced away from each other and then came back, repeating in quick three-quarters time.

He would, of course, possess a flawless baritone, deep and mellifluous and even, not the off-key, toneless songs she'd sung as a girl, back when there'd been funds for music instructors.

Oh, to have that money again, ill spent on a *venture* that had served no purpose.

As they faced each other in time to his singing, Connell brought her about so that his right hand curved about her waist.

"Th-this isn't the mazurka," she said, her voice breathless, that airy quality having little to do with their exertions.

"This is the original version. A gift from the Polish. Inspired by the horses of the Polish cavalry."

"I can see that." Her chest rose fast and quick. "N-never tell me?" They came together for the next one-set promenade in place. "Your travels?"

He grinned. "Exactly."

Since her brother had gone missing, she'd abhorred any and all thought of travel. She saw those jaunts and journeys to the Continent not in the casual light the rest of the world viewed them, but rather, with skepticism and mistrust. Only, here with Connell today, she at last discovered the pull that had drawn her brother away—and kept him wherever he was.

"Ta-ta-ta-ta-ta." Connell's wordless song became more boisterous, and a laugh burst from her lips as they raced with their own, running steps across the length of the ballroom.

His grin widened, highlighting that devil's dimple in his left cheek, the one that enticed and eased the severity of his otherwise harsh features.

She gave herself over to the dance. Not thinking about her article or her cello or her family's circumstances. Uncaring that Connell was Emilia's former betrothed. Instead, she simply let herself go with the happiness of the moment and how very wonderful it felt. And how wonderful it was to be in his arms.

Her stomach lurched.

All of her lurched.

Constance stumbled, her feet tangled with Connell's, and the weight of her and her skirts knocked him off-balance.

They came crashing down hard. His body broke her fall, and yet, all the air left Constance as she slammed into a hard wall of muscle no duke should have a right to.

They lay there, a tangle of limbs. Their chests rose and fell quickly, as in time as their steps had been moments ago. Constance lifted her head.

It was a mistake.

The tips of their noses kissed. Her breath mingled with his.

Connell's gaze dipped to her mouth, and his lashes swept low.

Her chest hitched. *He is going to kiss me.*

It was the last kiss she should want... and yet, she melted against him and angled her head in anticipation of his kiss.

A kiss that didn't come.

His hooded gaze remained locked with hers. The searing heat of that stare set butterflies loose low in her belly, fluttering and dancing about.

God help her for being weak for a roguish duke.

Constance pressed her lips against his.

Connell's body went still under hers, and then his hands were at her hips, anchoring her against him as he returned her kiss. This, each bold slash of his lips against hers... Nothing could have ever prepared her for... *this.*

It was the first time she'd ever kissed a man... or been kissed. Neither servants nor amorous gentlemen had ever attempted to steal that privilege, and she'd lived to believe that she would never know that passion. Only to find herself gloriously and blessedly wrong.

He licked the seam of her lips, teasing her mouth open for a further exploration. And curling her fingers into the lapels of his jacket, she let him have that. Wanting more. Needing more... of him.

She moaned as his tongue touched hers, a fiery brand that scorched her inside, fanning the flames of her desire. He tasted like chocolate and mint and honey, an unexpectedly sweet blend, not at all wicked and enticing in its purity.

And then, as quick as she'd begun it, he ended the singularly most passionate, glorious moment of her life. Her breath came in fast little spurts, and her lashes lifted as she tried to make sense of anything.

Then, through the net of desire cast by this man, horror crept in, that sentiment magnifying as a roguish half grin tipped the corners of Connell's lips up. "Now you can tell all your ladies the way to a duke's heart is through a lively dance set," he said, his voice rough with desire.

With a squeak, Constance struggled into an upright position, kneeling atop him. Her knee caught him square between the legs.

The air hissed between his teeth, and Connell rolled onto his side.

That abrupt movement sent Constance pitching onto the parquet floor. She caught herself on her palms. All the while, Connell writhed about behind her, moaning.

With all the aplomb Constance could muster, she stood. "That should not have happened, Your G-Grace." The slight tremor to that very last syllable managed to shatter her perfunctory, businesslike tone. "And I assure you it will not happen again." Though, with his piteous groaning, it was doubtful whether he'd heard that or… really any of what she'd spoken. "Now, if you'll excuse me?" She gathered up her things, stuffed them into her bag. "I will see you on the morrow." Not waiting for an answer, she made the never-ending march through his ballroom.

With every step that echoed around that mammoth room and followed her down Connell's empty corridors all the way to the front door and her merciful escape, she couldn't shake the fear that those steps they'd danced this day might not only be the way to a duke's heart… but to a lady's, as well.

CHAPTER 7

THE NEXT MORN, CONNELL SAT in wait.

That was not rhetorical, but a matter of fact.

His pipe gripped between his teeth and a copy of *The Gazette* open in front of his face, Connell sat on the narrow hall bench and read through the unlikeliest of materials—Mrs. Matcher's Guide to a Gentleman's Heart.

Granted, his reading had nothing to do with the content within and everything to do with the one responsible for the writing.

She really wasn't so very good at this. Not so much in the ways that would appeal to Polite Society, anyway. Nor would he, a failure of a poet, ever dare to pass judgment. Her advice came across as direct, almost listlike, and for his teasing yesterday, he found himself far preferring this directness to all the flounce and fluff stuffed into the *ton's* reading materials.

Dear Lost In London,

If you are in love, playing coy and disinterested isn't going to win you any gentleman's heart.

She came across as forthright and all-knowing, and Polite Society would despise the column for those very reasons. Connell grinned. That was also the very reason he'd found himself riveted by all the columns James had managed to procure since Constance had taken her leave yesterday afternoon.

In possession of several months' worth of her material, he'd an opportunity to appreciate that, though her advice had become abrupt and without the flair to draw in London's all-too-easily bored readers, he rather preferred the shift in her writing.

His brief and enjoyable interlude proved as short-lived as his every happiness.

"Not conventional, ye are," Jennie called from down the hall.

"Given the manner of housekeeper you are, I'd say that is the height of irony," Connell muttered to himself, directing that droll response into his pages.

The heavy clip of Jennie's serviceable boots grew increasingly closer until they stopped altogether before him.

With a sigh, he reluctantly lowered the newspaper. "Yes?" he urged when half of his household staff continued to glare at him.

She jerked a chin at him. "Dukes don't sit in their foyers."

"Servants of dukes don't call out their employers," he drawled. "And yet, here we are." Connell made to lift his pages.

"Ye ain't paid me for the week."

That brought his paper down once more. "I haven't..."

"Paid. Given me coin. Or James. We don't work fer free, ye know."

"And here I thought you were working for free spirits, food, and the comfort you've nabbed in the guest quarters."

Wonder of wonders, Old Jennie managed a blush. "It'd be a waste for the rooms to not go used. An' it's easier to reach ye should ye 'ave a need."

"Ah, why didn't I think of that?"

Their repartee was interrupted by a knock.

Connell and Jennie looked to the door.

Oh, bloody hell. She would arrive now.

Jennie, who didn't voluntarily take on any task, started for the door.

Connell scrambled to his feet. "Where are you going?"

"Oi'm openin' the door." The old woman eyed him oddly. "Ain't that what Oi'm supposed to do?"

"There's any number of tasks you *should* be seeing to. Why start now?" He softened that with a smile.

His housekeeper—or now it would appear, his all-purpose servant—scowled back.

Connell scrambled forward. In his haste to beat her to the oak panels, he stomped all over his morning reading. "I have i—"

Jennie had already drawn one of the doors open, revealing a befuddled Constance Brandley.

The lady lingered a moment on the stoop. "Uh… hello," she said when neither Connell nor Jennie spoke, and neither invited her in.

"Got nothin' for beggars," Jennie snapped, making to close the door.

Cursing under his breath, Connell shot a hand out, catching the door before it closed in Constance's face. "She is not a beggar," he said, in crisp tones. He motioned Constance forward.

The moment she'd entered, Jennie gave Constance a once-over. "Sure looks loike one. Oi dinna much about foine garments, but Oi'd say that is an old one."

Connell pushed the door firmly shut. "And even if she were a beggar, I trust that, given all you take, we can share some with others," he pointed out drolly.

"Bah," the old woman groused, slapping a hand in his direction.

Even with her hood drawn close, he caught the rustle of fabric as Catherine alternated her head back and forth, taking in the exchange. And no doubt, clever as she was, missing nothing.

"That will be all, Jennie."

"Ain't done with our discussion, we are." His housekeeper brought them back to the sole reason she was awake at this noon hour. "Me funds."

"Generally, the way this works is you receive an annual salary. Now, if you'll—"

"Don't know nothin' about that. Only know me wants me money." Jennie jabbed a crooked finger at the marble floor. "Now."

Reaching inside his jacket, Connell withdrew a small sack. "Here." He tossed it over.

With reflexes a cat would have been hard-pressed not to admire, she caught it in a wrinkled palm and peered inside. Her eyes bulged.

"I trust that is sufficient to keep you for some time?" he drawled.

Carefully tying the velvet string around the top, his housekeeper tucked her riches into her ample bosom. She hovered there, showing no signs of leaving. She gave a still-silent Constance another look. "Who's this one?"

Did he detect a snorting laugh coming from Constance? Surely not. Any lady would be close to tears and fleeing when presented with the noisy, insulting head housekeeper.

Jennie took a step closer. Six or so inches shorter than Constance's impressive height, the old woman peered up into the folds of that cloak.

Constance pushed her hood back.

The fearless minx. Of course she'd squarely meet Jennie's stare.

Connell closed his eyes and prayed for intervention from above.

"Hmph." Jennie crossed her arms at her ample chest. "Yer 'aving ladies to yer house now, are ye?"

"If I answer yes," he ventured with a droll edge, "would you promise to seek out a more *respectable* household?"

Old Jennie cackled. "Oi ain't interested in a respectable household."

Yes, given she and James had made Connell's sideboard theirs—and any other room theirs, as well—he could understand why.

Constance slid closer to the servant. "Does His Grace entertain very many lady guests?"

Oh, this was really enough. He opened his mouth to say as much, but Jennie proved quicker.

"'Ardly. Ain't that roight, Duke?"

Connell resisted the urge to rock on his feet. "I am a model of propriety where those social dictates are concerned."

"In… deed." By the way Constance split that word into two, she no more believed that than she did the world was flat.

Jennie scratched at her stringy white hair. "That ain't wot Oi meant. Oi meant wot Oi meant," she said in her thick Cockney. "And Oi think it's perfectly foine ye found yerself a friend, ye did?" Jennie beamed, smiling when he'd believed the harpy capable only of scowling. "Even if it is a lady friend."

Connell cleared his throat pointedly. "That will be all, Jennie." That crisp ducal command would have been enough to silence any servant, steward, or sovereign.

Alas…

"Oi told me James it was only a matter of time." Jennie's gap-toothed smile widened. She looked briefly over at Constance, who had her back blessedly to Connell, proving a small gift in light of the housekeeper's ramblings. "Not sure 'ow proper it is yer entertaining a lady, but better than yer being alone, Oi say."

Over the top of Constance's head, Connell shook his head furiously at Jennie.

Constance glanced back, and Connell abruptly stopped that frantic movement. He made a show of adjusting his cravat instead and briefly considered the mural overhead.

"Wot are ye shakin' yer 'ead for, Duke?" Confusion deepened the lines around Jennie's eyes. "Ye 'ave been alone."

Fire slapped at his cheeks. What had been an enjoyable day he'd found himself looking forward to had dissolved into… this… this mad Punch and Judy show. "I wouldn't say that." Not exactly.

Jennie snorted. "Then 'ow would ye say it?"

The glimmer went out of Constance's pretty blue eyes, ushering in a newfound sadness. He resisted the urge to cringe. The last thing he sought was her pity. "What Jennie means," he said, "is that no women visitors come calling."

His faithless housekeeper looked over to his very intently listening visitor. "In fact, none at all come 'round."

"Oh." It was a soft exhalation, no more than a sigh on Constance Brandley's lips.

He'd been wrong. The day had officially reached maximum capacity for bad. There was only one certainty—the afternoon couldn't get any worse.

"Where in blazes are ye, Jennie?" hard-of-hearing James boomed from down the corridor, and for once, Connell found himself welcoming the noisy man's intrusion. "Ah, the duke 'as company, does he?"

Connell slid between James and Constance, effectively ending Jennie's inquisition and James' examination.

James peered around him. "So this is why ye've been sitting in the foyer," the old man said slyly, shoving an elbow into Connell's arm. "Yer waiting for yer lady company."

Another lady—any *other* lady, that was—would have been run off in horror and shame. Constance, however, faced the dragon head on. "I assure you I'm not that manner of... er... lady company." She paused and then took a step closer. "I'm just... a friend."

"*A friend,*" Connell repeated.

He tested that word on his tongue and in his mind. In his thirty-five years, Connell had never kissed a friend the way he'd kissed this woman before him. And friends certainly didn't lust after each other, as he did. And yet, in a peculiar twist... he rather found himself enjoying her company.

"That will be all, James and Jennie," Connell said, and wonder of wonders, his pair of servants looped arms and without either a curtsy or bow to Constance or Connell, they ambled off, leaving silence in their wake.

Constance was the first to break it. "You... do have servants."

"Indeed," he mumbled. "Though the delineation seems dubious at best."

An entrancing little smile danced at the corners of her full lips. "Yes. That is true. They're quite unconventional insofar as servants go." She glanced down the path the old couple had taken, a bemused glimmer in her eyes. "Though I vastly find myself preferring that honesty and directness to the usual remoteness one finds amongst the family and the household staff."

It was an unerring and unnerving read on his very own thoughts where the servants were concerned, and Connell found himself silenced.

"You've been waiting for me?"

"I wouldn't say that exactly," he said for a second time that afternoon. If he'd wished to be absolutely precise, he would have said he'd been waiting for four hours and fifty-five minutes or so.

"Oh?" Her eyes twinkled as she looked away from his foyer seat and papers. "Then how *would* you say it?" she asked, borrowing Jennie's words. Not waiting for an answer, she headed for those messy stacks and dropped to a knee alongside them. She proceeded to rummage through the well-read articles.

"I had considered the possibility after our... exchange yesterday that you'd be scared off," he murmured, deliberately lowering his baritone. Connell took slow, languid steps over to her.

The lady didn't so much as lift her head. "Hmm?"

Alas, all these years of being reformed for the benefit of Iris and her mum had diminished all his roguish charm.

Undeterred, Connell strolled closer. He stopped directly before her so that only his morning reading stood between them. He waited.

And waited.

And continued waiting.

He'd be damned if he went from leading charmer to… invisible. "Or should I say," he purred when she remained engrossed in that advice column, "our stolen interlude?"

"Do you mean that kiss?"

Her droll amusement sent a damned blush climbing his neck and cheeks.

That kiss?

It was the singularly most unromantic way any woman had referred to his embrace. Ever.

"I assure you, Connell, it will take a good deal more to send me running than—" At last, Constance glanced up… and went absolutely still. Her gaze widened slowly until her eyes formed round moons. She swallowed noisily.

He tamped down a pleased grin. So he wasn't invisible to her, after all. "You were saying?" he asked in husked tones.

The brief lapse in her otherwise impressive control was almost instantly restored. Her arms filled, Constance struggled to her feet. "You are reading Mrs. Matcher."

"I have."

She eyed the piles a moment. "I'll have you know this"—she held one up—"is one of my older columns."

"That is reassuring, as the oldest material here left much to be desired," he said without inflection. Even so, he winced as the words left his mouth. Yes, all ability to charm had left him long ago.

Except Lady Constance Brandley proved a singular oddity in every regard. Her eyes brightened. "Do you truly believe so?"

He might as well have fetched her a star for the joy she radiated.

And he, who not even two days ago had sworn off all people, found himself reveling in being the one to bring this woman that happiness. At the same time, it was too much emotion for his jaded soul to know what to do with. "Shall we?" he said gruffly.

Her expression fell, and he instantly wanted to restore that previous light.

A short while later, they found their way to his office. Just as she had yesterday, she settled into the chair across from his desk and set herself up a neat little workstation.

While Connell fixed himself a drink, he studied her.

When he'd been younger, he'd kept company with the most outrageous widows and the unhappiest of wives in search of escape from the tedium of their own lives. All those exchanges had been sexual in nature. There'd only ever been one woman different than the lot before… Lady Emilia.

She'd been bubbly and bright… and innocent. That innocence had been so foreign that it had been a pull to his younger, jaded self. With Emilia, there had been sweet endearments and stolen kisses, but there'd never been anything meaningful. Not truly.

After just three days with Constance Brandley, Connell now knew that had been his fault. He'd not allowed himself to see Emilia—or really, any woman—in all the ways he should have.

As such, there'd never been a sparring of wits or debates. He'd not even considered the possibility that a woman would do something so unconventional among the *ton* as maintaining an advice column.

Constance had been honest about that from the first, and it was hard not to admire a woman who was not so proud that she'd turn her nose up at work—and more, enjoyed it. It stirred an appreciation that left him further disquieted.

This time when he carried his drink over, he didn't claim the same seat he did yesterday, but rather, the one across the sizable oak desk, putting that much-needed barrier between them.

She briefly lifted her gaze. "May I?"

"Of course." He gestured with a hand for her to carry on with her questioning.

A dimple appeared in her right cheek, and in a bid to focus on anything other than that appealing little puckering, he tossed back a swallow of his brandy.

"I was referring to a drink, Connell."

She wanted…? He followed her gaze to the glass in his hand and then looked up.

Constance's smile deepened. Who could have imagined that wide smile could have ever grown even more? "You're shocked."

"Hardly," he lied through his teeth.

As she glided to her feet and swept over to the sideboard, he stared at her retreating form and didn't bother attempting to hide his surprise. He assessed the lady as she picked up a decanter, studied it, and then set it down. She swapped that brandy out for another bottle. And another. Before settling on… whiskey.

"I just find it interesting, Constance." He dangled that enticement before her.

"That I like all spirits?" she countered. She answered her own question. "I don't like all of them." The clink of crystal touching crystal followed by the slow, steady stream of liquid pouring filled the room. Returning the bottle to its place, Constance turned, and one of her customary smiles curved her lips. "Just certain ones."

He found himself smiling… again. Because of her. Because of their repartee.

He shouldn't enjoy any part of this. Her, feeling again, being with her. Not when he'd resolved to live contentedly alone, and yet, there was nothing else for it. He liked being with her.

The moment she reclaimed her chair, he folded his arms and watched on, waiting for her to take the first drink. No one truly liked spirits. At best, one grew accustomed to the taste, but one never really preferred it.

Constance raised her glass and froze, the rim so close her lips brushed the edge, and Connell found himself envying that crystal. Her perfectly arched, thin golden eyebrows dipped. "You think I'm merely pretending."

"Bluffing. Pretending." Joining his fingers, he steepled them under his chin. "Either way, it's all the same."

Not taking her gaze from his, Constance tipped her glass back and drank, long and slow. The graceful column of her throat worked evenly before she set her glass on his desk. "You were saying?" A pretty flush stole across her cheeks, casting that cream-white flesh in a soft red, a hue to match her bow-shaped lips.

"What I'd intended to say is that you've identified another way a lady might find herself in possession of a duke's heart."

She dissolved into a paroxysm, choking on his revelation the way she hadn't his spirits.

Connell chuckled.

Constance glared at him through watery eyes. "You're just attempting to unnerve me."

"Have I? Unnerved you, that is?" he purred. "How very interesting."

"You're making light."

"I wouldn't dream of it," he said smoothly.

It was a lie.

He quite enjoyed teasing her.

But he'd also given her the truth.

CHAPTER 8

CONSTANCE WAS PLAYING WITH FIRE.

In fact, since discovering upon her arrival several days ago that her solitary duke was, in fact, the Duke of Renaud, she'd known as much.

So what was it that kept her here?

Mrs. Matcher's.

Her failing advice column, which Emilia had handed over to help Constance secure the funds to earn her cello back, *should* be the answer. And yet, she couldn't in all truthfulness to herself admit that remaining here was entirely connected to Mrs. Matcher.

She enjoyed being here.

And that was going to be what would leave her burned… if she let it.

Stop it. You're a thirty-year-old woman. Certainly past the point of worrying about scoundrels and rogues and rakes.

Constance eyed him for a long moment. That devilish half grin grazed the corners of his lips as if he refused to relinquish the whole of his smile. Cautiously, she set down her glass in favor of her notebook and pencil. "Very well, then. You're suggesting a lady who might earn your affections by partaking in spirits."

"Hardly," he said, not missing a beat. "I quite despise them."

She lowered her notes to her lap. "You aren't making sense, Connell." And he was no doubt being deliberately obtuse.

"Of course I am. Complete sense." He leaned forward. "It's not necessarily that I appreciate a lady who consumes spirits, but rather, what her doing so represents."

It was the first indication that he might, in fact, be serious and not just making light of her work for Mrs. Matcher. "What does that represent, other than scandal and wickedness?"

"Why is it scandalous and wicked?" he rebutted. "Because Polite Society has decided just how a woman should conduct herself. The *ton* would have ladies avoid spirits and wagers and hunting, and yet, they allow men those same pleasures."

That was an argument she herself had long posed to her parents, who'd lamented having a daughter who didn't conduct herself as a flawless debutante. From girlhood on to womanhood, she'd felt only resentment at the different and double standards to which the world held men and women. And now, here was a gentleman who felt the exact same way.

She searched for some hint that he jested... almost wishing it. Preferring that, because that version of Connell Wordsworth would be easier to face daily than the one who expected societal norms to be the same for men and women. "I cannot tell if you're being serious with me," she quietly confessed.

He shrugged. "Because you find it so hard to believe that a man might prefer a lady who thumbs her nose at societal conventions?"

"Because everything I've ever been told or learned speaks to the opposite of what you're saying."

"Trust me, love, gentlemen far prefer a lady with her own mind." Connell grabbed the pipe and a narrow tubing from his desk and proceeded to clean out remnants of ash and tobacco.

It was her turn to snort.

"You think I'm wrong?" he asked, filling the pipe and meticulously packing it.

Constance sat forward. "I know you're wrong." And yet, Constance had never been conventional by Society's standards, and that had not gathered her a single suitor.

His eyes sharpened on her face, and she instantly stilled. He wouldn't say anything. Yes, he'd a scoundrel's reputation, but he'd be too much of a gentleman to say—

Connell abandoned his pipe. "You're speaking of your own experience," he said softly. This time, his words were absent of his customary levity.

That somehow made her humiliation all the worse. Her cheeks went hot, and she damned her pale white cheeks, that curse of the English. Still, she sat up straighter. "I've raced and outridden gentlemen my family has had for guests through the years. I've sat at card tables and suggested we play hazard in lieu of the more respectable games. Invariably, those unconventionalities are met with horror." And she found herself unmarried and unloved by any gentleman.

"I never claimed I would provide guidance that was intended to trap some poor lady with a miserable, hopeless boor, Constance," he said. "What service would you be providing if you were doing *that*?"

Constance went stock-still, and her gaze slid past Connell's broad right shoulder. From the moment Emilia had offered Constance the opportunity to pen advice as Mrs. Matcher, Constance had thought about the funds she might earn. She'd focused on her ability—or rather, her inability—to appeal to the ladies writing to her in search of advice. But she'd not thought about *the ladies* so desperate as to put out a request for help.

Oh, she'd come to Connell's at a little girl's behest, but Constance hadn't considered changing the advice she was imparting to young women. Not truly. "You've a point there," she allowed in solemn tones.

The leather groaned, bringing her attention to Connell as he leaned closer. "As for you, Constance? If the only men with whom you've kept company can't appreciate a lady not cut from the same dull cloth as every other, then all that means is you've never met a gentleman worthy of you."

Just like that, a corner of her heart succumbed to Connell Wordsworth in all his charm.

The pencil slipped from her fingers and pinged upon the hardwood floor as Constance caught the inside of her lip between her teeth, holding on to her sigh.

The air came alive, as it always did between them. Around them. More terrifying now than it had been the day she'd first entered his household, because of the deepening intimacy between them.

Hurrying to retrieve her pencil, she fumbled about and put

several sentences on her page. "I... I believe I've everything I require for the day," she said, finishing off her notes.

When she looked back over to him, she didn't know what she'd expected. That he'd urge her to stay? And how, as she packed up, did she account for this disappointment that he didn't? That he instead returned to the casual act of filling his pipe.

After she'd tucked her things inside her bag, she made to rise.

"I was, you know, Constance."

She eyed him quizzically.

He nodded at the half-empty glass of whiskey. "Surprised at your spirit consumption."

Constance found herself smiling. "I used to sample my father and brother's stash of spirits before..." Her happiness faded.

"Before...?" he prodded.

She fiddled with the long straps of her bag.

This was new territory with him. Yes, she and Connell spoke of intimate topics. His interests, the ways to win a duke's affections. And yet, they'd not spoken much about themselves, their pasts, their families.

Their heartbreaks.

"My brother's long been a traveler. My mother always said he had wanderlust." For so long, she'd fought all memories, all thoughts of her brother. For now, she let them in. With this man. "In the summer, as a boy, Hadden would pack up his things and, before the sun was up, would set out, pretending he was exploring. And then he grew up." Sadness settled around her heart. "Protective as she'd always been, Mother *insisted* that he not travel. An heir's responsibilities and all," she said in a perfect mimicry of the countess." Constance gripped her bag so hard, her knuckles ached. "And I envied him. I envied him for being able to say, 'To hell with Mother and Father's requests,' and setting out anyway." Her throat clenched. "For going places he wanted, without a care for what Society would say." It was a heartbreak she'd not even really spoken to her friends about. Oh, they knew about his absence. But they didn't speak of Constance's worries. She looked up.

At some point, Connell had quit his seat and settled into the one near her, and for the agony cleaving at her chest, there was... a comfort from his being here.

"He's... been missing for nearly two years now," she said in a low voice. "My family had been searching since the last word from him came 'round." Spending funds they'd not had for information they couldn't find. That last part, she withheld. Some things even she was too proud to share.

Connell covered her hand, such warmth and assurance in that heavy grip. Slowly, almost of its own volition, her palm tipped up so their fingers were connected. And there was an absolute rightness in that joining. One that she could worry on after. Not now. Not in this moment. "I don't know where your brother is. I cannot tell you if he's safe or well, but what I can say? From just the small piece you've shared here, your brother loved to travel, and if something did happen to him, he spent the time he did doing something he loved."

Her throat clenched. "I am a selfish creature. His happiness doesn't matter more than me wanting him home," she whispered.

"No," he murmured, stroking the pad of his thumb over her palm. "It's the smallest of consolations, and yet, I've learned... after loss, it is important you take them where you can."

He spoke as one who'd also loved and lost. Did he speak of Emilia? Or his ward and her young daughter? Desperately, Constance wished for it to be the latter. Either way, they shared a bond that coalesced over loss.

Connell withdrew his hand, and she secretly mourned that latest of losses. Absently, he picked up her partially drunk whiskey and studied the yellowish contents. "I quite despise all spirits, you know."

He managed to surprise the sadness from her. "I..." She found her footing. "I didn't know. For you drink them so frequently."

"I've not been to any events in more than ten years." Then his eyes widened with a false surprise. "Never tell me you were paying attention to my drinking habits, love?"

Her mouth worked, but she couldn't utter a word, and then they all came at once. "No. That is, not in the sense you're suggesting." Years ago, she'd been wary about the rogue who'd captured Emilia's heart, watching him closely, though for different reasons than she did now.

"This time, I was teasing." Connell lifted a finger. "To your question, I *had* overindulged. My days of excess ended long ago."

"Because of Emilia?" This time, she couldn't stymie that question. The air hissed and snapped for altogether different reasons.

"I'm sorry, Connell. I shouldn't—"

He waved off her apology. "It's a fair question. That should have been the case," he murmured, more to himself. "The moment I met Lady Emilia, I stopped—" He cut himself short, and an adorable blush spilled onto his cheeks.

"Your dalliances?" she prodded when he still didn't finish his thought.

He gave his head a bemused shake. "Constance Brandley, you *would* have this discussion boldly and directly." And blast if another corner of her heart melted under those words she'd only ever take as complimentary. It was as though her frankness freed him. "But yes, to your point, I ceased my dalliances when I first approached her."

Her. Her stomach muscles tightened. Was he unable to bring himself to say the name of his past love? Was she even a past love? Yes, Emilia was happily married now, but that didn't mean Connell couldn't… and didn't still carry feelings for her. And why did that rapid spiraling of questions all bring her near to tears?

He swirled the contents of her glass in a smooth, slow circle. "I was loyal to her and remained so, but I still drank and wagered more than I ought. I didn't become a better man because of her, as I should have." He tossed back a sip and then grimaced.

Understanding dawned. "It was because of your ward."

He pointed a spare finger at her. "Yes, she was not my child, but having a babe about manages to change a person. Iris and her mother, Hazel, did that for me."

She waited for him to say more. When he didn't, Constance found herself left with new regrets: this hungering to know about the secrets Connell Wordsworth carried and to find out what these past years had been that had made him into this alternately sarcastic and somber gentleman.

This time when she made to leave, he didn't stop her.

CHAPTER 9

As a young man, Connell had loved horses.

The same way he'd abhorred spirits, he'd thrilled at riding his mount, particularly through the parks of London.

And yet, for the love he'd known for riding in Hyde Park, more than ten years had passed since he'd ridden there. At first, it was because Connell hadn't wished to. He'd neither a wish nor a need to return to London. There'd been nothing here but painful memories of a life that might have been. Eventually, that hurt had lessened, replaced instead with an absolute joy. His days had become centered on the happiness of the two placed in his care. From then on, there'd been even less of an interest in leaving the country for the bustling noise of London.

Now, he guided his horse through the entrance of Hyde Park in the heart of winter, at a time when he'd rarely—if ever—been here. Long ago, when he'd lived in London, he'd failed to find joy in anything beyond the heady pleasures. Of course, in his youth, he'd been no different than any other lord or lady of the *ton*. The moment the Season had ended and the cold crept in, he'd adjourned to his country estate, returning only when the revelries commenced.

As such, he'd never known it could be quiet in this end of England.

And the solitary person, more comfortable with his own company than any company, found himself welcoming the tranquility to be found here, after all.

How much he'd missed.

How much he'd lost.

The same familiar resentment swirled.

His breath stirred a little cloud of white, and only the rustle of an errant winter wind filled the grounds.

Connell guided his horse down a graveled path and didn't stop until he'd reached the shore of the Serpentine.

This was the spot.

The place where he'd come to the decision to offer for Lady Emilia Aberdeen.

If he'd wed her, they'd no doubt have been happy. Only, he'd thought to never again feel anything for any woman after her. The only emotion he'd thought he was capable of feeling for anyone had been reserved for the two who'd been placed in his care.

Only to find... he'd been wrong.

He was capable of feeling something for another.

And he didn't want to.

Restless, Connell returned his hat atop his head and dismounted. He looped his reins around a nearby oak and stared out at the thin coating of ice on the river.

Connell didn't want to take on another person's pain or worries. He was content living as a damned Elba unto himself. Because when you let someone in, they invariably destroyed you.

There was no other end result. Not for him. And, he believed, for anyone.

Knowing that as he did, Connell had formed a kindred connection with the unlikeliest of people—Lady Constance Brandley. For, at every turn, his life had taken him down a thousand different paths than he'd ever anticipated. From the moment he'd found himself saddled with a flighty ward and her child, to the speed with which he'd come to love that pair like they were his own daughters. But there wouldn't be daughters. Or a wife. Or any manner of family. Not anymore.

What accounted for that sadness? And why did it matter so very much?

As if to mock him in his melancholy, the far echo of laughter carried on a breeze, one voice deep and booming, the other light and airy. And also... distantly familiar.

Except, who did he know that would be here in London—?
The thought went unfinished.

Bloody hell.

Connell started quickly back over to his reins—too late.

The couple crested the slight incline at the very moment that he reached Cherish's side. Still afforded the coverage of the sizable tree trunk, Connell remained obscured.

Not that he need worry. The blissfully-in-love pair were wholly engrossed in each other. Their gazes locked, their smiles matching, they were joy personified.

Lady Emilia and Lord Heath.

His best friend and his former betrothed.

The discovery of their union had been a shocking one. She'd been vibrant, and Heath… well, he'd always been the more serious among his and Connell's set. They'd not seemed a match, in any way.

And yet, to an outside observer staring on, there could be no doubting the depth of their love and happiness.

And why shouldn't they be…?

As if following Connell's musings, Heath pressed a hand to the enormous swell of Lady Emilia's belly. Husband and wife looked down as one, moving in harmony as Connell never had with the lady… not truly. Together, the couple touched that spot where the babe rested.

And there was an unexpected rush… of red-hot envy.

Only, not for the woman before him, a woman he'd long, long ago given up on the dream of. But rather, for what she and Heath had, together.

It was the life he'd wanted: a blissful marriage. Babes. And now what was there?

His mount, the traitorous mare, tapped her hoof as if calling out a greeting to that jubilant pair.

Connell's former betrothed and his best friend looked up.

Bloody hell.

"Renaud?" Lord Mulgrave asked in disbelief.

Connell glanced about, more than half hoping the miserable father who'd not had time for a son about had returned and was, in fact, the duke now being called after.

Alas…

He stepped out from behind his cover. "Hello," he greeted, striding forward. He paused a yard away and, removing his hat, made a bow.

"Connell," his former betrothed said softly.

The last they'd seen each other, Connell had been attempting to renew their relationship, and she'd been pledging herself to his best friend. As such, there was certainly not a more awkward meeting than this one. "I… see congratulations are in order."

A blush pinkened Lady Emilia's cheeks.

"Thank you," Heath murmured for them.

Yes, of course, because commenting on a lady's indelicate state hardly fit with proper discourse. Particularly between ex-betrotheds and… whatever he and Mulgrave were.

"I hadn't realized you'd come to London," Mulgrave remarked.

"I'm… here," he said lamely. He'd quit the country for London, escaping the memories there. The irony wasn't lost on him. Unwittingly this morn, he'd rushed headfirst into the oldest parts of his past.

"And you've been well?" the other man went on, content to fill in the gaps in their friendship. But then, Mulgrave had always been the bigger man.

"I… have," he spoke with a hesitancy. Except, there was also a surprising degree of truth there. This had been the best he'd been in a long, long time.

Because of Constance.

Constance Brandley, who happened to be the best friend of the woman before him.

"And you both, I trust, are well?" Connell returned.

The couple shared an intimate smile that spoke volumes and required no words on their part to confirm what he saw with his own eyes—happiness.

His soul proved as black as it had always been, for he wanted that. He wanted to know all of that for himself. Happiness. Family. Love.

"We are," Lady Emilia finally murmured, her words more an

afterthought.

He expected to feel resentment at the loss of her, of this woman.

That didn't come. Rather, he felt bitterness at what he'd never have. "I have... matters to see to." No doubt Constance would be arriving soon. With that, he returned to Cherish and set to work untying her. Though it was wrong and completely inaccurate referring to Constance as *matters*. Not when she'd been the only scrap of light in months.

And there he'd gone again, attaching his joy to another person's existence.

Because, apparently, he'd not learned enough of a lesson two times—three, if one wished to consider his ward and her daughter separately.

Climbing astride his mare, he nudged the graceful creature from the copse.

"Renaud?"

Connell glanced down at the closest and only true friend he'd had in his life.

"I've missed you," the other man said. "Perhaps we might see one another again."

"I'd like that," he lied.

He was still deucedly bitter that Mulgrave had it all.

Turning his mount around, he rode from Hyde Park and didn't slow the mare's gait until he reached his townhouse.

Miracle of miracles, James stood outside in wait.

Swinging a leg over, he dismounted. "Well, this is a surprise—"

"Yer late," James snapped, taking the reins. "The lady is 'ere, and it ain't done to keep 'er waiting."

"I hardly need you to provide lessons on decorum," he snapped.

"Tsk-tsk. Miserable mood yer in. It'll be a wonder if ye don't scare off the lady."

"Where is she?" he asked, already climbing the steps and not glancing back.

"Jennie's taken 'er to the music rooms."

The music rooms?

Removing his hat and setting it on the foyer table, Connell found his way to the music room. As he walked, he unfasted the clasp at his throat, loosening it.

The haunting strains reached him first.

Flawless.

And full of such raw, powerful emotion that it brought him to a stop.

Seated on a gilded chair, with a cello positioned between her legs, Constance expertly plied her bow. Her chin tucked against the handle, her eyes closed, her head moved in quick time to her playing.

His breath stuck somewhere between his chest and throat, Connell caught a palm against the doorjamb and stared on as she played. Riveted. Awed.

He'd bedded any number of women. Widows. Actresses.

Not a single moment before this one had been as remotely erotic as Constance masterfully stroking a song out of that instrument.

Not a single moment had he been moved more than he'd been now.

Only, what she stirred with her playing wasn't solely sexual. It was an awakening inside him of so many emotions.

As Connell closed his eyes, his run-in with his past collided with Constance's performance. His life played out in time to that haunting melody, in a pace that matched her playing.

Every past pleasure he'd found… the people who'd moved in and then so very quickly out of his life.

It was a kaleidoscope of images that he couldn't bring himself to halt. Her music pulled each emotion he'd ever felt, magnifying it, sharpening them all so they existed in vibrant color.

So many mistakes.

So many losses.

So much of what would never be.

The smooth, melodic song came to a jarring, discordant halt that jolted him back to the present.

Connell's eyes flew open.

Constance's chair scraped noisily along the wood floor as she pushed herself to her feet. "Forgive me," she said, blushing. "You were late, and I… thought I might make use of your cello."

He waved off her apology. "You could have set fire to the room, and I wouldn't have cared or noticed." Or, that had been the case before he'd come in to find her playing. Something told him that from this moment forward, he'd forever see her as she'd been just moments ago, plying that quiver... And it terrified the everlasting hell out of him.

Even from across the length of the room, he saw the little frown upon her lips. "Your opinion of music, then, is one to be pitied, Your Grace."

Ah, she was displeased. Music mattered to her. Odd, he'd known her just a couple of days, and yet, it felt like forever. Her words merely served as a reminder of just how much of strangers they truly were. "You misunderstand," he said, starting over to her. As he spoke, his voice boomed around the music room. "It's not that I look unfavorably upon music." Nor would he ever be able to, given her siren's song of moments ago. "Rather, material things mean nothing." He'd come to appreciate that with the loss of those he'd loved.

Never the demure miss, she called back loudly and unapologetically, "You speak from a life of privilege, Connell. Sometimes, you don't appreciate what you have... until you lose it."

Her all-too-astute words brought the memory of Hazel and Iris whispering forward. The same melancholy that had dogged him that morning took hold. *Privilege.* The loss he'd known had been far greater, and from that pain, he'd come to appreciate how little any of this... mattered.

He reached her side, and as he considered the large cello she'd just played, he further loosened the clasp at his throat and shrugged out of his cloak.

Constance followed his stare and then hugged that quiver close to her chest, as if a protective mum prepared to battle for her babe. "I take it you... are a bit shocked at my choice of instrument."

It was not an unlikely opinion to form... by someone who didn't really know him. Polite Society had rules as to what was expected of young ladies, and seating herself at a cello would only ever be considered scandalous. He approved all the more because of it. "You still haven't gathered that I'm one who will only appreciate that which sets you apart from every other carbon copy of Polite

Society."

Her heart was never going to survive the remaining three days with him.

What was worse, she mourned that only two days were left following this one. She'd been so very content in her life, with her marriageless state and solitary endeavors, until he'd entered. From this day forward, she'd forever know what it was like to laugh and happily be with another.

Connell stood just a pace away. Close enough that the hint of winter air that clung to him filled her senses, dizzying and intoxicating.

And yet, as much as his words won a piece of her heart, they proved sparse.

Why was he not speaking? In the short time they'd spent together, she'd come to gather that he freely engaged in all discourse, from witty repartee to somber discussions, as he had just yesterday when they'd spoken of her brother.

Then, he'd been tender and kind and also insistent in his views of Hadden's decisions… and loss.

Now, he stood before her a remote, vague stranger, just as he'd been when he'd opened his own front door to her days before.

"My mother and father never really approved of my playing," she said in a bid to break the stilted awkwardness between them. She moved into position behind the cello and lovingly stroked the grandly crafted piece from the flamed maple ribs to the spruce neck. The deeply varnished instrument fairly gleamed in the sunlight that streamed through the windows. "They hid the cello. Moved it from room to room and insisted I play the pianoforte, or the violin, even. And then one day, they accepted that I'd not quit searching for it and brought it back to me." That had been the last time she'd separated from her cello until they'd been forced to sell her instrument.

Material things mean nothing…

And yet, having lost everything, she appreciated the gift each item and artifact was. The memories attached to them.

When Connell didn't respond, she stopped trying to fill the void of his silence.

"What was it?" he asked finally, his gaze on the magnificent cello she'd availed herself to.

"Antonio Vivaldi's *L'inverno*."

"*Winter*," he translated. He didn't look at her. He just continued to stare on at the string instrument. His lips twisted in a cool grin so very different than every other smile to come before it. "How very perfect," he said with a bitterness so tangible it nearly singed.

Warning bells tinkled distantly at the far corners of her mind, and she noted those details that had failed to escape her before this moment. The harsh lines of his mouth. The distance in his gaze. "You are upset."

"You've not done anything to anger me," he said tersely.

Fiddling with the bow in her hand, Constance drifted out from behind the instrument. "I wasn't speaking about me having upset you. It was more a general observation that something has."

"What reason have I to be upset?" he asked, spreading his arms wide. His cloak, draped over his left forearm, swept the hardwood floor. "I've no responsibilities. No entanglements. Nothing to worry about."

Perhaps had she not come to know him these past days, she'd have believed in the image he attempted to sell her on now. The detached scoundrel content with a carefree existence.

Not any longer.

For she did know him now. And it was why she knew his former charge had been so very right. Connell, the Duke of Renaud, was so very lonely.

"Do you... wish to talk about it?"

"No," he said before the offer had fully left her mouth. He paused. "Unless you are merely offering for the sake of your column."

She frowned. "You needn't be rude." It was a state she'd not seen him in, neither years ago when he'd been the always smiling future bridegroom to Emilia nor as the droll rogue who'd allowed her entry four days ago. "And as you've said, I'm not the cause of your foul temper. Something—"

"Someone." He chuckled, the sound harsh and guttural and

empty. "Though it might be fairer to say someones." With a restlessness to his movements, Connell wandered to the pianoforte and tossed his cloak atop the gleaming instrument. "I had the pleasure of seeing Lady Emilia and her husband, my best friend... my former best friend."

Her heart missed a beat.

She searched for some response. Any one that might be suitable. Any one that might be merited.

And failed abysmally. "Oh." His foul temper was because of seeing Emilia, then.

Why did that realization leave her so very bereft?

Because you care for him. Because you've come to enjoy being with a man who encourages you to be yourself and speaks candidly to you about anything and everything.

The idea that he was still torn up with regret and longing for Emilia left a hollow ache in her chest.

Neither could she be resentful of his feelings after seeing Emilia. There was no helping how a person felt about another. Constance spending time with and caring for the Duke of Renaud—her best friend's former betrothed—was proof enough of that.

She found her footing. "I trust... it is hard to see that." But still, she could not bring herself to say aloud the name of her best friend, the woman responsible for Connell's upset. "Them, together," she clarified slightly and then winced. Her words would only bring him further pain.

"It's not seeing her," he gritted. "She's married. Long ago, I set aside my feelings for her. I've accepted that and her choice of husband."

"Is it possible to simply set aside feelings for someone?" She put that forward as a gentle question. "Because if the heart is engaged, I don't see that one can ever truly be free of that pain, Connell."

Because when they went their separate ways, she'd mourn and miss him and their time together. What must it have been... what would it always be for him... with his feelings for Emilia?

A sound of frustration escaped him. "It's not about Emilia," he insisted, dropping the pretense of formality and owning the intimate connection he'd once had—still had—to Constance's best friend.

"I don't see what else it could be about, Connell."

"It's the life I gave up," he exploded, bringing her up short. He began to pace, slashing his hands wildly as he walked. "It's a life I *should* have."

"With her—"

"For the love of all that is holy, cease with the mentioning of Emilia." His voice soared and echoed around the music room. "I gave up everything. I should be the one with a family. With little babes underfoot, mischievous boys and girls turning me gray."

"You wanted a family," she said softly. And the children he spoke of... not a ducal heir, or the requisite spare, but rather, boys and girls. Ones who were not the well-behaved ones Constance's own parents had desperately sought to make her and Hadden into.

"I trust that is something else hard to believe." Another harsh laugh shook his chest. "The scoundrel duke longing for a family of his own."

Her heart melted and then cleaved in two for what he'd lost... and what he wished for.

"But... there can be that, still," she said gently, laying a hand on his forearm.

"You and your romantic mind with your damned romantic column," he cried, jerking away from her and stealing away the slight connection she'd forced between them.

Constance let a shaky hand fall back to her side and hid her palms in her skirts. "It's not simply about being romantic—"

He scoffed, cutting into her defense. "How to win the heart of a duke? How to win the affections of some lord who likely doesn't want to have his damned heart engaged, because no good can come from it? No good *ever* has."

He was scared and scarred, and his willingness to own that vulnerability sent a tenderness swirling in her chest. "But you can be happy again." That was what she'd come here to help him see.

"I'm not so foolish as to tie my happiness to another person." He gave his head a disgusted shake. "I'll not make that mistake. Not again."

Not when he'd already lost... not once, but twice. If the ghost of Emilia hadn't been barrier enough between Constance and a future with him, that jaded vow to never let someone in was reason enough that there could never be anything between them.

The earth ceased turning on its axis while she was left there, unsteady, her mind spinning. Her body swayed ever so slightly, and she shot her fingers out. They found purchase on the smooth pianoforte. The cool grounded her and gave her strength. It wasn't about what she might wish could have been between them... but rather, what he could have in the future. With someone else.

That was why she'd been sent here at a little girl's request. Focusing on that, Constance stretched her other hand out. "You'll not ever be happy if you insist on keeping walls up about you, Connell. By not trusting, by fearing you'll be hurt again and shutting yourself away in your grand new townhouse, you only stand to lose."

He stared at her fingertips, and for a moment she thought he might take them in his. For an even longer moment, she ached for that touch.

That didn't come.

"I already lost," he said tiredly. "I sacrificed—"

"Yes, you did," she said insistently, her self-control breaking. "You *did* sacrifice. You gave up Emilia for your ward and her daughter, and that was your decision, and if you hadn't? You would have never known the time with the little girl who came to matter so much to you. The little girl who still worries after you." Perhaps there should be concern in revealing that truth to him. And yet, she wasn't one for lies. Even those of omission.

And perhaps, if he couldn't shake himself from this quagmire of isolation for himself, he could do so for the child who'd brought him to this point.

He stilled. "What do you know...?"

"I know... some of what you're feeling," she said quietly. Reaching inside her bag, she found the heavily creased note that she'd read so many times, the words, long memorized, had already begun to fade from the page.

Connell took a lunging step forward and grabbed it. His eyes made quick work of the page.

He looked up. Fury burned from his eyes. "That's why you're here," he seethed between gritted teeth. "To help the wounded, broken, lonely duke." Even as the latter two words left him, Connell cringed.

The implications of this proud man being exposed registered. "No," she said quickly, giving a frantic shake of her head. "That isn't why I'm here. I mean, in a sense, yes, but not in the sense you're suggesting."

Crumpling the letter, he balled it up and tossed the wrinkled scrap to the floor. "Get out."

She jerked. Of every response she might have expected to meet her honesty and concern, being tossed from his properties had not been one of them.

But mayhap it should have been.

Constance tried again. "She loves you and is worried after you."

"She has her own life." A dull flush splotched his cheeks. "And I don't need anyone's damned worrying after me," he thundered.

Constance jumped.

"I don't want your pity, and I don't want your prying."

She jutted her chin up a notch. "I've never pried."

Leaning down, he stuck his face close to hers so the tips of their noses touched. "And why should you? You've already gathered everything you needed to know about me from my former charge."

They remained locked in battle, both their chests rising and falling quickly.

The air shifted, still charged and angry, but the undercurrent of desire and raw passion that was always between them surged a degree.

His gaze fell to her mouth.

Constance's lashes swept lower, and she tilted her head back a tiny fraction to receive his kiss.

A kiss that didn't come.

"We're done here, Constance," he said tiredly, snapping the spell, and she hated that her body and heart both screamed out for the loss.

She'd not, however, be sent away. Not so easily.

Constance caught his hands, and when he made to pull away,

she held firm, tightening her grip. "I've never been in love, but I have loved and deeply. As such, I know what it is to lose someone that I love. To wake up every morning thinking they're there, only to remember all over again that it will never again be." His facial muscles rippled, and she softened her tone even further. "But there can be life after a broken heart, Connell."

"You're assuming I want that," he said, his voice flat, his words running through her. A perfectly placed spear that he couldn't know found a mark.

"I don't know what you want," she brought herself to say. "But I have to believe it's not this solitary life, shut away from the world, that you now live."

His lips twisted in a macabre rendition of a smile. "You don't know me, Constance Brandley. Stop presuming you do. The only reason you're even here in the first place is because of Iris. Likewise, the only reason I've shared anything is because you came here looking for information for some silly column."

Her entire body jerked.

He was trying to hurt her.

Because he was even now hurting inside.

And yet, that did nothing to lessen the effects of his blow or soften the rage sweeping inside. Turning angrily on her heel, she stalked over to her bag, swept the satchel up, and started past him.

Waiting for him to stop her.

To apologize.

To say something.

Anything.

When he didn't, her hurt melted away, replaced with a far safer, white-hot anger. Constance whipped back around. "You're a coward and a hypocrite."

He sputtered. "I b-beg your pardon? I have never—"

"It is true. Not even a day ago, you spoke to me about my brother. You insisted I find some solace in knowing that his decisions were what brought him to that moment." She swept forward, her skirts snapping angrily about her. She slammed her bag down and dug her heels in. "Well, I'll tell you, Connell Wordsworth, the same way—the exact same way—my brother made decisions that brought him to his fate is the same way you've come to this moment in your life. And so you can be angry and bemoan the unfairness, but you owned those choices and for a while? For a while, you had happiness with your ward and her child..."

"I don't want to hear—"

"Of course you don't want to hear it. It's far easier bemoaning your fate and not being called out for it. You might not wish to hear this, but you'll listen anyway," she shouted over him. "Your ward and her daughter are still here. You can still see them. They've not died." They'd not gone missing as her brother had. "You can still know happiness with them. You're just *choosing* not to."

His nostrils flared, and his lips worked, but no words came out.

Which was fine, because she had words enough for the both of them. She jabbed a finger at him. "Just as you're choosing to be alone and shut away, feeling bad for yourself."

A hiss exploded from between his teeth. "Get the hell out."

"I'm already leaving," she snapped, hurrying to gather up her things.

"We're done here," he called after her.

"And here I'd thought that's what 'get the hell out' implied, Your Grace."

Except, as she stormed out, pausing only to don her cloak, she couldn't fight the tears that blurred her vision.

It was done.

What was worse, this misery had nothing to do with the unfinished research for her advice column and everything to do with the fact that she'd never again see Connell Wordsworth.

CHAPTER 10

THE DAY CONSTANCE BRANDLEY LEFT was a happy one.

The second day after her explosive departure, Connell celebrated her absence. He had precisely what he'd wanted—quiet. Not peace per se, but blissful, much-longed-for silence.

It was the third day when he registered just how very quiet it, in fact, was without her.

Nay, this had nothing to do with being alone… or wanting just anyone about.

Rather, it was that Connell missed *Constance*.

Seated at his desk, with his legs propped on the corner of it and his untouched pipe between his fingers, he studied the same half-drunk whiskey that rested beside his heels. The dusty snifter there, but not forgotten. It couldn't be forgotten if he stared at it day in and day out. Had there been a proper household staff, some maid would have seen that article cleared and the tangible memory erased.

But then, in leaving Sussex to escape thoughts of his ward and her charge, he hadn't really ever shaken himself free of those memories. They lived on, the moments shared and experiences that had come.

What he had failed to appreciate, however, was just how quick one might build memories with another person and the void that could be left after even a fleeting connection.

She'd not been deserving of his anger, and he'd had no right resenting her for being in his life because of Iris. Nay, he should have appreciated her all the more for it.

He'd wronged Constance's best friend, and he'd been such a self-absorbed bastard during that courtship that he'd not even paid attention to the most important of details—such as the names of Lady Emilia's friends. For those reasons alone, Constance could have very well ignored Iris' appeal the moment she'd come to realize just who Connell, in fact, was.

But she hadn't.

Your ward and her daughter are still here. You can still see them. They've not died. You can still know happiness with them. You're just choosing not to.

In the heart of his own bout of self-pitying, he'd failed to see the truth in her words as she'd accused him of licking his wounds.

As such, since her departure, Connell had come to appreciate that he didn't much like how he'd behaved toward Iris. Toward Hazel.

And toward Constance.

Was it a wonder that she'd not come back?

Why should she have wished to return?

A sharp, angry knock sounded at the door, jolting him.

Connell's feet skidded off the side of the desk, as with that furious rapping, hope stirred in his chest.

His feet hit the floor just as James opened the door and stepped inside.

Connell's heart leaped.

And then promptly fell.

"Ye got company," James snapped. He jerked his thumb at the well-dressed, bespectacled figure beside him. "This one. Said ye were expecting 'im?" It was an angry demand for an answer, and at any other time he'd have been amused by that angry challenge from his peculiar butler.

"I now understand the urgency of your summons," Mr. Downes said in his nasally tones. He adjusted the leather folio in the crook of his right arm and looked down his nose at James. "I… can see you're in need of proper household staff."

The butler surged forward. "Ye snobby bast—"

"That will be all," Connell said quickly, coming around the desk. For a moment, he thought James intended to go after the smaller, more severe man anyway. But then the servant smoothed his heavily wrinkled lapels. "Preferred yer other company"—he tipped his head at Downes—"to this one."

Yes, Connell had, too.

The moment James had gone, Mr. Downes dropped a bow. "Your Grace." He glanced from the dusty glass back to the panel James had slammed in his wake. "As I said, I now understand the urgency in your summons. Please rest assured I can rectify this situation *immediately*."

This situation. That was how the obedient servant would refer to James.

How many would act the same way Downes did even now? Not once had Constance ever been so condescending and rude to the unlikely servants, and blast if he didn't find himself missing her all the more.

"I'm not concerned with my household staff at this moment," he said, motioning to one of the chairs. "I summoned you for different purposes."

Except, as Downes slid into the leather folds and set about making himself a neat little workstation at the corner of Connell's desk, Connell stared on. In that seat, he saw another. One with enormous, out-of-mode skirts and an equally ancient notebook and tiny little pencil clutched between her fingers as she'd recorded every word Connell had uttered. Like a dutiful student, she'd been…

Until she'd spoken, and challenged him, and killed any such illusions.

For the first time since she'd left, a smile creased his lips.

Downes stared questioningly over, and Connell got to the reason why he'd summoned his man of affairs. As Connell spoke, Downes scribbled notes in his book.

Not once did he pause to ask questions. Theirs wasn't a real engagement, not really. Connell dictated, and Downes listened on as the obedient servant. Because that was how the world responded to Connell as the duke.

Constance had never treated him so. From the moment he'd opened his door, she'd challenged him… and he'd never appreciated that frankness for the gift it was, until she'd gone.

When Connell finished, Mr. Downes glanced up from his notebook. "Is there anything else you require, Your Grace?"

Connell gave his head a clearing shake. "I don't want any expense spared," he said. "And I'd like the matter attended to with some urgency. Is that clear?"

"Yes, Your—"

The door opened, and Connell and Mr. Downes looked as one to the entrance.

A scowling James ducked his head inside. "Ye found yerself a new butler, 'ave ye?" James snapped.

Mr. Downes' spectacles slid forward, and he pushed them back into place, his eyes rounding.

"I beg—"

"Oi didn't realize until Oi left and Jennie pieced it together why this one is 'ere. To be yer new butler."

Downes sputtered. "I am certainly *not* a—"

"Because Oi expect me an' moi Jennie to be treated better. Oi expect if yer goin' to sack us, ye 'ave the courtesy of—"

"I'm not sacking you," Connell interjected.

From across the desk, Mr. Downes muttered something that sounded very much like, *I'd highly suggest you rethink that.*

Shoving the door hard, James stomped over. "Wot was that?"

Mr. Downes cowered in his seat, the notes in his hand fluttering to the floor.

"James," Connell warned, and his peculiar servant turned that scowl on him. Connell gave his attention back to the quaking servant. "We are done here." That sprang the man of middling years to his feet.

"Damned straight ye are," James snapped as Mr. Downes hastily gathered up his things.

"I will see to your request," his man of affairs vowed. Dropping a bow and cutting a wide path around James, he left.

As soon as he'd gone, James stormed over. "Wot did 'e want?"

"It's none of your affair. However, let me assure you your role here is safe."

His butler stared suspiciously back and then grunted.

"Now that you've confirmation that you and Jennie's work here remains unchanged, I trust there's nothing else you require."

James frowned. "That ain't why Oi'm 'ere."

Of course it wouldn't be. "I've just paid you—"

"Not that, either," James said impatiently.

"Then—"

"This missss." Jennie's loud whisper came from the hall.

Connell's heart clamored once more in his chest. She was here.

That fledgling hope was given another death knell by James.

"Jennie is of the opinion that ye need to go an' apologize to the miss."

It was the manner of outrageousness that would have appalled and shocked all of Polite Society—a duke being given directives by his servants.

Alas, well-meaning servants.

For all their bluster, they were good people.

Jennie stomped into the room with Connell's cloak all but curled in a ball. "'Ere," she said, throwing the garment at him.

Connell caught the article against his chest. "What is—?"

"Ye don't get to run a lady off," Jennie interrupted. "Go give 'er yer apology. We don't work for rude masters. Paid a boy to 'old yer 'orse." She paused. "Thinking it moight be wise to 'ire 'im on permanently."

"Please do," Connell said as he shrugged into his cloak. "You are the housekeeper, after all."

The old woman preened, but then her scowl was firmly back in place. She grunted. "Go on." She swatted Connell's arm.

"I'll have you know," he said as he latched the clasp at his throat. "I was intending to make amends for my behavior." Or, he'd known he should.

Jennie snorted, that inelegant noise calling him out as the liar he was.

Some fifteen minutes later, after a quick ride through the empty streets of London, Connell found himself handing his reins over to a boy lingering around the front of the Earl of Tipden's. "I'll be along shortly. If you could care after her?" He tossed a small velvet sack.

The boy caught the purse in his dirty fingers. "Sure can," the boy promised, covetously eyeing the funds.

Connell started up the steps and paused.

You speak from a life of privilege, Connell. Sometimes, you don't appreciate what you have… until you lose it.

"If you're interested in work," he said to the boy, "I'm looking for help in my household."

The child's eyes formed wide circles. "That would be splendid, sir."

Bounding up the remainder of the cracked stone stairs, Connell lifted the knocker and announced himself.

There were several long beats of silence.

A winter wind whistled in the morning still. Connell rubbed his gloved palms together in a bid to bring warmth into his chilled hands. Had anyone been in Town for the winter, his presence here would raise all manner of questions and scandals. Not that Connell was one who cared much either way what the *ton* had to say.

When several more moments passed and no one came to answer, Connell took a step back and looked up. He peered at the tightly drawn curtains without so much as a faint part in the fabric. The manner of closed-up curtains was when occupants had gone.

The oddest little pit formed in his belly.

She'd left.

Her family had likely departed for their country seat. As it was, she and her family had remained far longer in London than most members of the peerage did.

Regret swarmed him.

Regret for how he'd treated the lady, not because he cared about her.

His stomach lurched, and his skin went hot and then returned to its previous cold state before going warm once more.

Cared about her?

Where in blazes had that idea come from? He cared for her only as much as she was Lady Emilia's best friend and… and…

Liar.

The door suddenly opened.

A slightly out-of-breath, wizened, little old man greeted

Connell, and as Connell handed over his calling card, he didn't even attempt to make himself believe he wasn't relieved that the Brandleys remained. When the ancient butler made no offer to issue an invitation inside, Connell cleared his throat, more than half fearing he'd been correct in his earlier assumptions about the Brandleys. "I'm here to see Lady Constance."

As the butler scanned the card, his gaze froze on Connell's title.

The man's sizable white eyebrows went shooting up. The coarse-looking hair touched a tousled head of unkempt white hair to match. "Please come inside, Your Grace."

The moment Connell stepped inside, a small servant in ancient liveried apparel to match Constance's dress came forward to accept Connell's cloak and hat.

Connell noted an interesting detail. The Brandleys had their own eccentric household staff, which, given Connell's crew of two, was saying a good deal indeed.

"This way, Your Grace," the old butler murmured with a deep bow and a click of his heels that proved, however, just how different Connell's ragtag servants were from even this unorthodox pair.

An eager restlessness filled him.

Of course, she'd not be pleased with his presence. They'd parted under the most ignoble of circumstances, with him an ogre, ordering her gone and yelling after her the whole way of her exit.

The earl and countess' butler suddenly lurched forward with an alacrity Connell would have bet his estate the old man had lost some twenty years earlier. The old man hastily pulled a door panel closed, shutting away the inside of that room.

But not before Connell caught the sparse furniture, a lone sofa and an armchair, in the otherwise empty parlor.

Over his stooped shoulder, the servant shot a suspicious look back at Connell.

Connell swiftly concealed his features, masking all of the surprise.

As he was led on, however, his eagerness to see Constance was set aside as he instead noted additional details, such as the faded gold wallpaper that had brighter places where frames had once hung.

All the muscles of his gut clenched and unclenched.

"Here we are," the butler murmured, opening a different door and ushering Connell inside.

He did a glance around—the drawing room.

"I shall see Lady Constance is informed of your appearance." With another bow, the butler limped off, and Connell was left alone to his study.

For a moment, Connell believed his eyes had failed him earlier. Mayhap he hadn't seen what he'd thought he had.

For all intents and appearances, this drawing room might as well have been any other extravagant one in London's finest homes. Gilded frames lined the wall. The pair of King Louis XIV chairs and arched sofa were elegant and classic in their lines and design.

And yet...

Wandering deeper into the room, Connell noted details he would have likely otherwise failed to note had it not been for that empty parlor he'd passed on his way in. The faded fabrics. The ancient curtains.

Connell stepped before the fireplace mantel.

It was the chill. An absolute chill permeated the room, a product of a stone-cold hearth.

Reflexively, he rubbed his gloved palms together in a bid to bring warmth to them.

And now, it all made sense. Constance seeking him out. Her advice column. Her out-of-mode garments.

You speak from a life of privilege, Connell. Sometimes, you don't appreciate what you have... until you lose it.

And he, who'd jilted one woman and given nothing but silence to his ward and her charge for carrying on with their lives, had believed himself incapable of stooping any lower and being any more shamed than he'd been in his thirty-five years... only to find, waiting for Constance, how very wrong he'd been.

CHAPTER 11

"HIS GRACE, THE DUKE OF Renaud, has arrived and requested a meeting with Lady Constance."

It was hard to imagine that a sentence could usher in a greater screeching silence.

Curled up on a sofa, with her knees drawn close and a blanket tossed about her shoulders in a search for warmth, Constance sat, absolutely frozen.

Certain she'd misheard the butler in the doorway.

After all, it was altogether possible he was mistaken. It wouldn't be the first time Scott had shown senility.

Bypassing his employer snoring away in the corner, the old servant looked between Constance and her mother.

"*Who?*" the countess yelped, her voice creeping up a decibel.

Constance's father snorted himself awake. "Wha—who—?"

She sighed. Alas, if Constance had misheard, that could only mean that her mother had misheard, as well.

Scott swallowed loudly. "His Grace, the Duke of Renaud," he whispered in his ancient, drawn-out tones as the earl had fallen asleep once more.

The countess sailed to her feet. "Whhhhhhaaaaaatever is he doing here?"

Constance's father jolted awake again. "What is—?"

"Shh." It was a sign of the desperation of the moment that both Constance and her maid, Dorinda, both attempted to silence the countess.

When her mother again spoke, she had the wherewithal to speak in a quiet, but still outrage-laden whisper. "Whatever is he doing here?"

"Whatever is who doing here?" the earl asked, with as much interest as he showed his wife when she spoke of her needlepoint projects.

"That bounder," her mother exclaimed. "That libertine. That... *rake.*" Suddenly, her eyes lit, and a slow-dawning horror took root in Constance. She was already shaking her head. "That... *duke!*"

In but two words, hope was born in the countess' tones.

Constance closed her eyes. "Mother," she said warningly.

There'd been a time not very long ago when the countess' status would have trumped all, including a visit from a disgraced duke.

"Desperate times and all that," her mother said. Rushing over, she took Constance by the shoulders and gave her a light shake. "The Duke of Renaud is here to see you."

Her father's heavy brow wrinkled with confusion. "To see who?"

The countess slashed a hand in Constance's direction. "To see your daughter."

"I cannot imagine why," Constance said softly. That much was true. After their volatile parting, she'd never dared to expect to see him again. And she'd been bereft at the idea of it. Just as she was unable to quell the light giddiness in her chest at knowing he was here.

Scott coughed into a fist. "Should I say Lady Constance is not receiving—?"

"No!"

Like denials exploded from both mother and daughter.

A guilty flush heated Constance's cheeks as her mother chose that miserable moment to turn a sharp gaze on her. "Oh?"

Father scratched at his slightly balding pate. "But... I thought you thought we should turn the bounder out."

"He's not a bounder." The defense slipped out before she could call it back. Constance bit the inside of her cheek, hard.

Her mother gave her an even longer look, and Constance fought the need to shift.

"That is..." Constance couldn't come up with a single, justifiable explanation of her defense without revealing the fact that her new opinion of Connell came from having spent intimate moments with the gentleman, alone. "I expect I should see what has brought His Grace to call."

Of course, there would be questions after. But for now, there was a reprieve.

Her mother beamed, and Constance could all but count the guinea signs as they flashed in her eyes.

Once, she would have seen that response only as ruthless and unforgivably disloyal. As a woman whose brother had gone missing and as a woman who'd gone without fire in the winters and had had scarce meals, she'd come to appreciate that, in terms of humbleness and humility, desperation changed a person.

Her mother patted at her coiffure, and her features were immediately smoothed into a mask more reminiscent of the one she'd donned years earlier, when Constance had been a girl and had believed her mother couldn't be anything but unflappable. "I think that is a wise idea," the countess said in perfectly even tones. "Don't you, dear heart?" she asked her husband.

A snore met her query.

That crafted façade was immediately shattered when Constance made for the door, and her maid started on her heels.

"Halt there!" the countess squeaked, bringing both women's gazes over. "That is, perhaps you should rush along, Constance, and Dorinda might… see to refreshments."

"There aren't refreshments," Constance said, exasperated.

Her mother strangled on a fit. "Shh!" she chastised, gripping her throat. Through water-filled eyes, she glared at Constance. "Have a care," she mouthed.

Constance began the trek to the lone furnished parlor in their residence.

She gave her head a shake. Yes, because Constance stating the truth of their family's financial circumstances was vastly more egregious than her mother sending her only daughter on to entertain a gentleman. Alone. A gentleman whom the Countess of Tipden had disparaged for years after Emilia's shattered betrothal.

Though, in fairness, you were also in possession of a like ill opinion. And had it not been for a little girl's letter and Constance's visits with the gentleman, she still would have had the same unfavorable thoughts.

But he was nothing like she'd believed him to be.

In any way.

She'd never have gathered he was one who didn't expect a woman should be any one way.

Or that he, one of Society's most notorious scoundrels, should long not for wicked pursuits, but a family.

And she'd never have known he was vulnerable, a man who was hurting.

Because of his charge and her daughter…

And Emilia, that voice jibed, reminding Constance that, ultimately, Connell would always be a man longing for the woman who was Constance's best friend.

She stopped on the edge of the parlor and took a moment to smooth her hands along the front of her hooped skirts. And then stepped inside.

Connell stood at the empty hearth with his hands clasped behind him.

Constance's heart did a funny little leap.

She'd missed him.

Of course, these past days without his teasing company, she'd known she had. She'd missed their repartee and those discussions about her brother, ones she'd never had with anyone. Not even the women she'd called friends since she was a small girl.

But until this instant, seeing him here, she'd not realized just how much.

His tall frame went still, and she knew the moment he registered her standing there.

Just as she registered him at the cold hearth and the implications of his being here and the state of her family's circumstances. Constance and her family had been clever enough to keep that secret from the world, but Connell was clever enough to note details others had otherwise missed.

She balled her hands tight at her sides. "Hullo, Your Grace," she said quietly as he turned to face her.

His features were smooth and even as he passed that impenetrable gaze over her. "Constance," he murmured, not bothering with the pretense of formality that she'd put up between them.

It was a thin barrier.

And he'd kicked it thoroughly down with that piercing stare.

She ventured deeper into the room, taking up a place alongside the ivory upholstered sofa. "Would you care for refreshments?" she offered and promptly held her breath until he shook his head.

"No," he added, and then with those sleek, panther's steps, Connell joined her.

She waited until he'd seated himself before claiming her seat.

Connell drummed his fingertips along the arms of his chair. "How very formal you are, Constance."

Constance leaned close. "What did you expect given our last exchange, Your Grace?" she said in hushed tones. "Did you expect I should assume we would be teasing and light and—"

"I'm sorry." His quiet apology brought her words and thoughts to a screeching halt.

The experiences she'd had with, well, anyone, really, had revealed that most people were too proud to apologize. "What?" she blurted.

A small smile ghosted his lips, and drat her heart for dancing to the beat strummed by this man's charm. "I'm sorry," he repeated, and then his grin faded. "When we last met, I was atrocious, and you were undeserving of my displeasure. There is no explaining it, nor would I be so bold as to ask you to pardon such behavior, either."

"I…" It was the most beautiful, most eloquent apology anyone had ever given her. And him, a duke, a step from royalty, should have made it. But then, he wasn't at all the aloof, self-important peer she would have taken one of his rank to be. "You were hurting," she finally said.

He made a sound of protest and waved a hand. "That doesn't give me or anyone reason to behave as I did."

"Is that why you've come?"

"It was."

Was? Her heart sped up. For that slight distinction in tense suggested something had changed, and perhaps she wasn't the only one in her madness who wanted the company of one she had no business wanting.

"I found myself wanting to take part in your column."

Of anything he might have said, of anything she would have expected, that admission had certainly not been it.

Then…

Connell's eyes slid to the empty hearth. It was the barest, ever so slight fraction of a shifting of those thick golden lashes.

Had she blinked, she would have missed that telltale gesture. And yet, since the moment she'd entered the room and found him here, she'd been riveted by him in all his golden glory.

Constance stiffened.

For she knew.

She knew that his offering didn't come because he truly wished to help her, or even because he missed her.

Missed her as she'd missed him.

Nay, that offer had come because he knew.

And despite everything Emilia or Society or even she had believed of him as a dishonorable scoundrel, Constance well knew now how wrong she'd been. Yes, he'd made mistakes in how he'd ended his betrothal and not sharing his reasons for doing so, but those mistakes didn't make him dishonorable.

A different fluttering hit her belly. Shame. A sizable pit.

His expression dipped. "You are… speechless, I take it."

Constance plastered a smile on her lips. "No." She clipped that single syllable out between her teeth.

His eyebrows went shooting up. Apparently, that had not been the response he'd anticipated. A frown tugged those magnificent lips down at the corners. "I… No?"

"I thank you for that offer, but I believe I've sufficient… material." Moments she'd written in a notebook, taken from their all-too-brief time together. "As such, I must politely decline." Constance jumped to her feet. How was it possible to both want a person instantly gone and also be riddled with sorrow over the thought of their leaving? "I thank you for coming, and I appreciate your apology."

He scowled, and with a languidness, Connell stood and began a slow walk toward her. "You're upset."

"N-no." The stammer made her a liar. His ability to gather, after knowing her just a short while, precisely what she was feeling made her unsteady.

He stopped when all that was between them was the ancient King Louis XIV chair. "Here." He dusted the tip of a finger between her eyes. "The inner corners here draw in and then up when you're upset."

Oh, God. He knew that. How did he know that? She didn't even know those nuances of her facial reactions, and yet, Connell, the Duke of Renaud, should?

"And here, your lips come down." Her pulse hammered erratically as he stroked a bold finger along the corner of her mouth. "And your jaw goes up."

If he could read those minutest of responses and gathered those sentiments, then everything in Constance told her this man, this wicked scoundrel, with his rogue's charm and his eyes that saw too much, need only just glance at her to know the effect his presence had on her. That he knew that, she hungered for him, against all better judgment and reason.

Dampening her lips, she took a hasty step away from him. "I know what you're doing." At the dangerous half grin that curved his lips, heat slapped at her cheeks. "That is, with regards to your offer."

His brows dipped. "I don't…"

"I know that you know, Connell," she said on a frantic whisper and immediately stole a glance to the doorway, because surely it was only a matter of time before her mother took up a place at that doorway to get to the bottom of whatever took place in this room.

He followed her stare, and when he again spoke, Connell matched her hushed tones. "That is absolutely untrue."

"Isn't it?" She crossed her arms. "*Isn't it?*" she repeated for good measure.

The hard slash of his lips flattened into an even harder line.

Constance said it anyway. "You've deduced that my family is in dun territory."

When she uttered those words and the door didn't come bursting open was when Constance had all the confirmation she needed that her mother wasn't listening at the panel. Because horror would have sent her flying in here. And yes, Constance likely, too, should have been besieged by that same sentiment—she'd admitted to being impoverished.

Only, somehow, she'd shared more and was more comfortable with this man than she'd ever been… with anyone.

That was why she'd come to him. That was why she was Mrs. Matcher… and why she'd sought him out.

Shame sat like a stone in his belly.

"It is why you write the column," he murmured.

He proved to be very much the bastard the world knew him to be, for he found a gratefulness that she'd come into his life. Had she a fortune and never taken on Mrs. Matcher's column, he'd never have known her. He'd never have known a woman named Constance Brandley, who bowed a cello to rival the angels in the Lord's celestial symphony.

She hesitated and then slowly shook her head. "That is why I've taken on the column. At first, it merely represented an opportunity to earn some coin." His insides hurt, thinking of her struggling in any way. "A chance to purchase back my cello."

He'd believed his heart completely broken two times before this time, only to have it ground into pieces beneath that unwavering, matter-of-fact admission.

"Your family sold your cello," he repeated, his voice graveled and rough. Even he heard the sharp edge there.

Constance heard it, too, for she frowned. "It was one of the last items they were forced to trade to creditors." They were undeserving of the defense. "I know what you're thinking."

"You don't."

"You blame my parents."

"And you don't?"

"They aren't wastrels, Connell. My father isn't one of those dissolute lords who squanders coin at the gaming tables. My mother never insisted we hold on to useless baubles and pretty trinkets."

He thought of the bare halls and empty rooms he'd passed. This sparse parlor.

No, the lady was correct on that score. Her family wasn't living beyond their means, as so many lords and ladies in debt were wont to do. The pieces of the puzzle slid into place. "Your brother," he said quietly.

"My parents… we have been desperate for any word of my brother. They've chased any hint or story of him." Constance hugged her arms about her middle. "Sometimes, I think the not knowing, this lifetime of wondering, might, in fact, be harder than…" She shook her head. Those words went unfinished, but their meaning was clear. Sadness darkened her eyes, and the need to draw her into his arms and hold her close was a physical hunger. To offer the embrace that she now offered herself. She suddenly let her long limbs fall to her sides. "I enjoy it," she said, bringing them back to the matter of their debate. "Writing the Mrs. Matcher's column," she added for clarity. "It is something I'm not necessarily the best at, but I find pleasure in it."

Had she been anyone else, he'd have believed she searched out compliments. "You still have no idea how vastly preferable your direct manner of writing is." Vastly superior to the supercilious, flowery prose of her predecessor.

A pretty blush filled her cheeks.

Connell caught her hand and brought her knuckles to his mouth. "Continue to meet with me," he urged and then touched his lips to her gloveless fingers.

"I said I don't want your—"

"This isn't about pity." How could she believe he felt anything other than respect and admiration for her? How many men and women of the peerage would have sooner cut a limb off to save a fortune than take on work?

"Did you ever truly wish to help me with my column?" she shot back on a whisper. She didn't allow him a chance to answer. "Or was it really about making light over it and having fun with it?"

Constance tugged her hand free, and he yearned to link their fingers once more.

Connell caught her lightly about the arm, staying her, keeping her there, close to him. Where she shouldn't be. But he wanted her there anyway. But then, he'd never been one to do that which he was supposed to.

"You are not wrong…" He grimaced. "That is… you *were* correct, Constance." Their gazes locked. "There was an element of cynicism on my part. A large degree of it, but it wasn't long before I enjoyed…" Her breath caught, and he moved his eyes over her face. *Being with you.* "Our talks," he finished, the words true, but not complete in how he felt.

She opened her mouth, but he pressed two fingers against her lips, halting the words. "It's not pity," he said with a quiet insistence. "You have helped me far more than I've helped you, and if Iris saw benefit in us working together, then it could only be right."

Constance remained silent for a long while, and he braced for her rejection. He didn't want to think that this was the end of their time together. Only because she represented a diversion from the dreariness that was his life. That was all it was.

"Very well," she said softly, holding her fingers out, and the slight lifting of his heart made a liar out of those earlier assurances.

"Of course," he said, laying his palm in hers and agreeing to terms that brought him to smile.

"We've two more days."

Two days. That effectively killed Connell's grin. He'd come here, wanting her back in his life for the remainder of their agreed-upon time, which was just two days. "Was it… just two lessons left?"

"It was… is." Did he imagine the wistful, almost sad quality to her confirmation? Or did he merely project his own miserable sentiments in that moment?

"Tomorrow, we meet in Hyde Park," he murmured.

"Hyde…?" Three little endearing lines wrinkled her brow, and he brushed a finger over them.

"At eight o'clock on the edge of the Serpentine." With that, Connell forced himself to stop touching her… and left.

CHAPTER 12

"BUT WHAT DID HE *waaant?*" Constance's mother pressed for the thirtieth time since Connell had taken his leave yesterday.

Shrugging into her cloak, Constance did what she did best where her mother was concerned—she deflected. "Who?" she asked, latching the clasp at her throat.

From the corner of her eye, she caught the grin on her maid's lips, and Constance winked.

The countess emitted a huff of annoyance. "*Who?* Who else would I be talking about?" She looked to Dorinda and then moved closer to Constance. "His Grace," Mother said in an egregiously loud whisper.

"Ah. I already told you, Mother," she said with a like exasperation.

Her mother furrowed her brow, and as Constance started for the door, her mother followed quickly after. "You *did?*"

"I did," she lied.

"I don't think you did," the countess said, speaking to herself. "I'm certain that I'd remember something so very—"

And God bless Scott for waiting at the door so she could make her escape. "Good afternoon, Mother." Constance gave a wave and set out with Dorinda close at her heels.

"Where are you going?" the countess cried from behind her.

"To Hyde Park."

There, at least, she'd offered her mother a truth.

"But… but it's freezing out."

Constance scoffed. "I'd hardly say it's freezing."

Except, as Scott drew the oak panels open, a gust of wind

whipped through the foyer, making a liar of her. Constance forced a smile. "See? Pleasantly warm for the winter, it is."

Scott closed the door on her mother's sputtering, and Constance hastened down the steps for the waiting carriage.

A short while later, having left Dorinda at the ancient conveyance with her sweetheart, the driver, Constance found her way through Hyde Park.

Her teeth chattering, she rubbed her palms together. The old gloves, thin from wear, did little to keep the chill out. And yet, even with the wind making a tangle of her skirts and biting into her skin, she couldn't contain the excitement that ran through her. At seeing him. At being here, alone with Connell Wordsworth, the Duke of Renaud.

As she recognized it was pointless trying to lie to herself, she owned that eagerness. Oh, she didn't seek to convince herself that it was in any way right.

And yet...

Would Emilia truly blame Constance? Emilia, who'd fallen in love with Connell's best friend?

Even if you had Emilia's blessing, that would do nothing to erase the fact that Connell himself would be forever enthralled by his first love. Nor had Connell given any indication that he even wanted more *with* Constance.

But he did enjoy being with her. He'd said as much.

"And you're being pathetic," she mouthed. Constance stomped up the rise that looked down at the shore of the Serpentine and immediately found him there.

A solitary figure in midnight black, a stark mark upon an otherwise gray landscape.

She paused and devoured the sight of him: his broad back, his long legs encased in fawn breeches that hugged heavily muscled limbs.

She sighed. Is it a wonder she or any woman would fall to a puddle for this man?

Only...

The wind caught the strings of her bonnet and sent them whipping under her chin.

This appreciation for Connell went beyond more than the physical... or the feel of his mouth on hers. There was a kindred connection with this man, where she could speak freely, without censure and without care that he might judge her, because he never judged.

Connell turned, and doffing his hat, he waved it toward her.

Even with the fifteen feet between them and the slight rise, she caught the smile on his lips.

Lifting her hem, Constance skipped down the hill.

Skipped. When was the last time she'd moved with such exuberance?

Surely it had been as a girl, plotting and planning with her friends on how to win the heart of a duke.

Constance stumbled as that old memory came sliding in. She fell and tumbled over herself, rolling down the hill, also as she had as a girl. Those times, however, had been intentional.

She grunted and came to a stop at the bottom and looked up.

Connell grinned down at her. "I used to love doing that as a boy." He held a hand out, and she stretched her fingers up, joining their palms as one.

In one effortless pull, he drew her up. She fell into his arms and remained there, wanting to stay there forever.

Alas, he immediately set her away. "Come now," he urged, tugging her onward.

How did he still not realize she'd follow him anywhere?

"Who did you go tumbling down hills with? Do you have siblings?"

He shook his head and didn't break stride. "Alas, my parents were dutiful to all Society's rules, but failed to adhere to the requisite spare."

She could imagine him as he'd been, mischievous and troublesome and even wilder than he was as a grown man. That only reminded her of how much of this man remained a mystery.

He'd also offered a glimpse into his past. "They were endlessly proper, I take it?"

"They took their ducal and duchess responsibilities with a greater seriousness than the king took his royal ones, I always said."

Constance searched the beautiful planes of his face for some indication of what he was feeling. "Was yours... a lonely childhood?"

He slowed his steps, and his brows came together. "I was never alone. Society would never dare leave an heir to a dukedom alone. And certainly not my parents." A wry grin formed on his lips. "No matter how much I might have wished for it." He gestured with his hat as he spoke. "There were always plenty of people underfoot. Tutors and instructors and solicitors and men of affairs, all people who'd one day answer to me."

Constance stopped, and Connell came back around to face her. "That's not the same thing," she said softly. "Being with people is not the same as being *with* people."

His expression grew wistful. "No. No, you're right on that score."

"Hazel and Iris," she supplied, knowing him enough now to gather just how much that beloved pair had shaped him.

"I didn't realize how solitary my existence was until them. I never knew the difference, as you pointed out," he clarified. "From my days at Eton and Oxford and then after, I surrounded myself with so many people, but I didn't realize until much later that those people weren't really friends and were certainly not family. I'd only had one true good friend," he murmured, and they resumed walking.

"Lord Mulgrave."

He nodded.

"I... trust that will always be hard for you," she said softly. "I am sorry for that."

Connell scoffed. "Don't be. I've told you, I regret how I handled the dissolution of my betrothal, and yet, I don't regret not being with Lady Emilia."

She chewed at her lip. Those thoughts weren't compatible.

"You're thinking that doesn't make any logical sense," he hazarded as they started for the Serpentine.

Constance huddled into her cloak, "A-a bit." The winter chill lent a quiver to her words. She was also thinking that another person being able to read her unspoken thoughts would never be anything but unnerving.

"If we'd wed, we would have been happy, until someday when she realized that mayhap there was another man who was better for her. A man who made her smile in ways I didn't and be free in ways she wasn't around me. And that man would have been my best friend." He gave his head a wry shake. "Imagine how very miserable each of us would have been, *then?*"

"That… is certainly a way of looking at it." A way she'd not considered.

"Heath is her soul mate in ways I never was."

"I don't…" Unfamiliar with the term, Constance shook her head.

"Soul mates," he repeated. "Two people with a lifelong bond. It is the strongest one a person can know. Coleridge recently wrote of it."

She was reminded all over again that he'd a love of poetry and was a wordsmith.

They reached the shore and stopped. A large leather sack lay atop a boulder. Briefly distracted, she glanced at the bag. "What is this?"

"Why, I thought that should be apparent, given the nature of our relationship."

What was the nature of their relationship? It was all confused now in her mind.

And worse, in her heart.

"We're on to the latest lesson for your column."

The latest lesson.

"And… what lesson is that, Connell?"

"Ice skating, of course."

He'd not even bothered to ask whether his betrothed enjoyed skating. In fact, he didn't really know anything about her.

But he knew what this woman's smiles meant. He knew the many meanings of the tilt of her lips.

This latest grin to curve that full mouth was the one he preferred on her—unrestrained and filled only with joy.

Constance laughed, her breath stirring a little cloud of white.

"Ice skating."

"I trust you're familiar with the pastime?"

She gave a little flounce of her golden curls. "I'll have you know I'm *quite* skilled at it."

He reached into the bag and pulled out a pair of blades.

Constance's laughter filled the empty grounds of Hyde Park, bouncing off the winter still. "You're mad."

Since the moment he'd drawn his first breath, born into the role of future duke, he'd been met with deference for no other reason than because of the title that would be his. "Have you called me... mad?"

Her features settled into a mock-somber mask. "I am. Mad to the extreme, you are, Connell Wordsworth."

Mad.

He rolled that insult around. The lads at Eton had been obnoxiously fawning. Had a single person ever dared treat him... as any other man? It was a refreshing way to go through life, and he hadn't known he'd been missing it until Constance had stormed through his front door and into his life.

"Ah," he said, holding the smaller skates aloft. "For the things we have to learn before we can do them, we learn by doing them..." When she made no move to take the blades, he pressed them lightly against her until she was forced to take them.

"Whoever said that?"

"Just now? I said it."

With her spare hand, Constance gave him a swat.

"Aristotle," he said. "I might have paid attention to my Greek lessons." Connell perched himself on the boulder and proceeded to strap one of the skates over his boots.

"Well, either way, I already know how to skate. Therefore, I needn't an experiential lesson."

"Ah, but I'm not referring to your learning to skate," he corrected, holding a finger up. "I'm speaking of the ways to win my heart."

He teased and set out bait that was met only with silence.

Lifting his head, Connell looked up at her.

High color had flooded her cheeks. It had rushed in quick and had nothing to do with the cold. He paused. "I was teasing," he blurted. "I wasn't really suggesting that I want you to win my heart."

"Oh, I know," she said quickly, her words tripping over themselves. "I didn't think you were. I—"

They spoke over each other, their words tumbling together. "Because, of course, you don't want to win my heart," Connell said.

"O-of course I don't." Her teeth chattered. "Th-that would be… imprudent and—"

"This is all for Mrs. Matcher's."

"Wh-why, of course it i-is." Another bell-like laugh spilled from those lips he yearned to claim once more. "Why else are we here, after a-all?"

"Precisely. And why would I want your heart?"

As soon as the words left him, he wanted to pluck them back.

That unintended insult brought Constance up short. She ceased rambling.

"Either heart," he blurted.

Constance tipped her head, sending her bonnet tumbling sideways.

"That is, why would either of us want one another's heart?" *Stop. Talking.* "Not just yours." *Just stop.*

And then, one of them managed a brief pause in talking. Constance claimed a spot on the boulder beside him, seating herself at his shoulder so their arms nearly brushed. She began to pull on a skate.

Neither of them spoke.

To each other, that was. Constance muttered under her breath as she struggled to hold up her skirts and don her skates.

I wasn't really suggesting that I want you to win my heart. Because, of course, you don't want to win my heart.

As Connell adjusted the straps of his skates, he cringed inside. Good God, when had he become so very useless around women? He'd once been seductive and had an ease in speaking to women. He'd been charming, damn it. *Charming.*

Only, something told him this woman was different. Connell stole a sideways glance at her as she struggled with her hem, cursing in the quiet. Something told him that had any other lady been beside him, he'd find the right words and never stammer—or worse, accidentally insult her. Yes, he'd be lying if he didn't acknowledge there was a hungering for her there. That since she'd lifted her head and boldly kissed him back, he'd yearned for more.

With her, he spoke freely about everything, from matters of jest and heartbreak to an assessment of Society's double standards. And here he'd thought himself capable only of cynicism and anger.

Standing on his blades, he knelt before her.

Constance shot him a questioning look.

"May I?" he murmured.

She hesitated a moment, before relinquishing the skate.

Connell caught the edge of her skirts and froze. His pulse hammered faster. All because of exposing her ankle. He lifted her hem.

Lust went bolting through him. Head bent over that tantalizing flesh, Connell closed his eyes and struggled to rein in his desire.

For an ankle. A damned ankle.

Granted, a decidedly delightful one that her thin leather boot contoured, accentuating the curve of—

"Are you all right?" she asked, jolting him back into movement.

"Fine." It wasn't the first lie he'd given her.

"I'll have you know there's nothing wrong with your heart."

"Thank you," she said drolly.

He winced, searching hopelessly for any of that rogue's compliments that had once come so effortlessly. Connell sank back on his haunches. "I'm making a mess of this."

Constance leaned over. "Actually, I think you nearly have it on."

He closed his eyes briefly, his shoulders shaking with silent mirth. "I was referring to my words."

She paused. "Oh. Yes, well, you are correct on that score."

A laugh burst from him, and she joined in, and how wonderful it felt to laugh with another person. Nay, not just with anyone. With her. *This* woman.

He came up on his knees and palmed her cheek, hating the glove that denied him the satin softness of her skin. He searched his gaze over her face. "Some gentleman will be so very fortunate to win it." Except, those words ushered in an image of some faceless stranger. A man wholly undeserving of Constance Brandley's wit and courage and strength. And Connell wanted to thrash the unknown bastard within an inch of his life… and then finish off the job.

"I'm thirty years old, Connell," she said without inflection and with matter-of-fact pragmatism. "My days for besotted suitors have come and gone."

And she'd been left unwed. "Well, no one said cold Englishmen know a thing when it comes to matters of the heart." With the life he'd lived, Connell himself had proven as much.

Her lips parted ever so slightly.

Unnerved by all that potent emotion blazing from those revealing eyes, Connell set to work on her skates once more. "Come," he urged when he'd finished, not wanting anyone or anything between them. He stood and took her hands, guiding her up onto her feet.

Together, they ambled back to the shore and onto the ice. Hands linked, they glided their way over the frozen river.

The scrape of their blades cut through the winter quiet as they moved in harmony, farther out, away from the shore.

Constance broke away and pushed herself ever faster over the ice, skating around him, over and over, in circles that left him dizzy. But then, that was the effect Constance Brandley had had upon him from the start. She moved as gracefully upon the ice as she did the steps of a mazurka, and he stopped to just admire her.

As she skated, the warmth of her breath left a little cloud of white in the winter air.

"For someone who professes to w-wishing for a l-lady who might s-skate, you're doing a rather poor imitation of it yourself, Connell Wordsworth," she called over, her voice carrying in the still.

Because he wanted to remember her as she was in this moment, and to move was to shatter that…

Constance skated quickly back over and then ground her blades to a halt, kicking up ice upon the otherwise smooth surface.

Her chest rose quickly, and then wordlessly, Constance gathered his hands in hers and urged him forward.

He'd been wrong. There was something even more magical than watching her in motion… It was joining her.

They didn't speak for a long while, the scraping of their skates and the errant winter wind the only sound between them.

"I forgot how much I enjoyed this," he murmured. Where just days ago there would have been only misery in thinking of the little girl he'd taught to skate, now there was a return of joy.

"My brother adored the summer," Constance said suddenly, an unexpected shift in discourse. "He loved fishing and riding and swimming. We were alike in that regard. It will always be my favorite season." It was another detail she shared that he tucked away to preserve forever so that when she was gone, he might remember everything he could about her. "The first summer he was gone, I hated the green of the leaves and the lush grass and the blue skies. All they did was remind me of him and more… his absence." Constance glided to a slow halt, bringing Connell to a stop before her. "But do you know what I realized, Connell?"

He shook his head.

"Hating what I once loved because I missed him only left me empty. The beauty of summer, it reminds me of him. And I prefer a world where I at least have his memory rather than nothing at all."

Her words moved through him.

All this, while he'd chosen to feed the darkness and sadness instead of retaining the joy that Constance had allowed herself to find in thoughts of her brother.

Connell cupped a hand about her nape and angled her head back so their eyes met.

The sough of their breaths mingled in the air. "Thank you," he said softly.

She smiled, those crimson rosebud lips moving up and bringing his gaze downward. *I want to kiss her. Here in Hyde Park. Uncaring if anyone rides past.* Nothing mattered but tasting her once more.

"D-don't thank me, Connell," she said, her teeth quivering.

He'd been wrong.

Something did matter more.

She was cold. He'd urged her out, in the dead of winter.

Her body trembled, a reminder of the winter's cold, which ushered in the remembrance of her family's empty hearth.

Suddenly, a lesson in the outdoors proved the most caddish and inconsiderate of ideas.

"Tomorrow," he murmured, drawing her hood closer about her, "can you sneak away to my residence?"

"I-I've done it four times before," she said with a bravado he admired and brought a smile to his lips. "For our last lesson."

Her eyes were stricken. Or mayhap that was his own visage reflected in her clear gaze.

"Our last lesson," he murmured.

As they resumed skating, the earlier joy was lost to the sobering reality that five days would never be enough.

CHAPTER 13

The following morn, James escorted Constance through the halls of Connell's home.

For her final lesson.

Their last lesson. Their very last one.

She wanted to cry.

And she likely would have had it not been for the loquacious servant given to curt utterances.

"Worried ye moight not come back, Oi did."

"Did you, now?" she asked the refreshingly candid butler, and she welcomed the diversion from her thoughts.

"Oi did. And we'd be left with the surly lordship… once more."

She studied this angry-looking servant given to muttering and cursing. "And I take it you don't care for working for an ill-tempered duke?"

Not breaking stride, James scratched at his head. "Oi don't give a rot if someone has a foul mood, but 'Is Grace ain't been happy. Those are different things."

Her chest tightened. "So it is… His Grace you're concerned about?"

He scowled, but didn't deny that supposition. "Any other lord woulda 'ad us locked up in Newgate for invading 'is 'ome. The duke, 'e not only gave us a place to stay and food in our belly, but the finest posts in his household."

That was the moment when Constance realized she'd never be the same. That, regardless of logic or loyalty of friendship to Emilia or honor or dishonor, she'd forever be in love with Connell

Wordsworth, the Duke of Renaud.

"'Course," James went on with no apparent indication that Constance's entire universe had been rocked upside down, "from the start, Jennie an' oi, we thought surly was his only disposition."

She slowed her steps. "And has he been… very surly?"

"Before 'e met ye? Or after ye left?"

Constance paused. "Either time?"

"Both times." James moved closer. "Miserable 'e was, until ye arrived."

Her heart quickened. Until she'd arrived.

It's not pity. You have helped me far more than I've helped you.

What did it mean that he'd not been miserable after he'd met her? Aside from that day when he'd spied Emilia and her husband, that was.

It was a sobering and much-needed reminder that she had no right to any thoughts of longing where Connell, the Duke of Renaud, were concerned. For Emilia. And as important: because of Emilia, too. Connell might have felt bad for how he'd treated Constance after his meeting with the happy couple in Hyde Park, but it had also proved a stark warning that his heart belonged to another.

Constance made a show of adjusting her satchel strap. "I… trust it's merely a coincidence."

James snorted. "If ye think that, ye ain't as clever as me or me Jennie 'ave taken ye for."

"What are we talking about?"

With a shriek, Constance spun about.

Connell lounged with a shoulder propped against the wall. The negligent pose would have made debutantes and the oldest of dowagers swoon and sigh. Constance found herself no more immune to that devastating appeal.

He winked.

"Connell," she blurted. She strangled on the last syllable of his name, her cheeks burning up. "That is," she said in more measured tones, "Your—"

"Save it. Never understand ye fancy sort, unable to say a person's given name," James muttered as he stomped off. He threw an arm up in the air as if in disgust, and that managed to diffuse the tension of the moment.

Constance smiled. "I like him. I like the both of them."

"They like you." Connell's grin widened. "And I didn't think they cared for anyone. Not even each other."

"They care about you, too," she said, and a blush marred his cheeks. This powerful duke and societal scoundrel blushed at the idea of his servants caring about him.

That brought her back to the little girl who'd written to her, asking for Constance to help bring him happiness. "We should begin."

With a sweeping gesture, he motioned for her to enter. "After you, my lady."

As she stepped inside the room, she restlessly fiddled with the feather she'd tucked into her hair that morn.

Constance didn't want to like Connell. She preferred her thoughts ordered and clear.

There were certain, inalienable truths she'd trusted as fact: Connell, the Duke of Renaud, was the scoundrel who'd broken her best friend's heart. He wasn't to be trusted because of it.

As such, Constance could have never anticipated how very right the young girl could have possibly been about the gentleman being sad and solitary and… not so very awful.

Not so very awful, at all.

And it scared the bloody hell out of her.

It also, however, served to remind her that they were linked only because of Constance's column and the little girl. And that after today, there'd be no reason to again come here. He'd allowed her five days, and this was the fifth… and her heart ached for the very reality of it.

Stop it. Rechanneling her focus back where it should be, Constance sat down and rummaged around her back for her notebook and pencil. When she had them out on her lap, she looked at Connell. "Now—"

"Ah, all business again, are we, love?"

Love. Her cheeks warmed. Nay, her entire body did. And butterflies swarmed around her belly, from nothing more than his husky endearment. Yes, *all business* was how she had to be if she had any hope of holding on to some of her sanity and a scrap of her heart when she left him. "That segues us nicely to today's meeting," she said crisply.

Connell leaned forward and rested an elbow on his desk and then his chin atop his palm. "Are you certain you wouldn't care for a glass of whiskey first?"

"I'm quite sure. I'm not an overindulger, Connell."

"That's not a word," he pointed out.

She scoffed. "Well, it should be. People indulge, so why is it not possible to overindulge?"

A study of contemplation, Connell tapped his chin a moment. "Fair point." There was a beat of silence. "Though, I'd hardly call you an overindulger, as you haven't had a glass in several days."

She waggled her eyebrows. "Not that you know of."

He grinned his devil's grin, and she silently cursed herself for engaging in their usual repartee.

Constance tapped her pencil on her empty page. "I want you to tell me what it is that would make a young lady fall in love with you."

Why did the idea of her giving guidance to some other lady on how to win his heart alternately make her want to weep and wield her pencil like a dagger at this nameless stranger?

Because you love him. Even after just a few short days. Even as it is wrong and defies logic. And the idea of him with anyone else destroys you.

"I thought we were working on your column, not on the state of my love life."

"They're linked," she said with a little toss of her head. That gesture was ruined when her feather slipped over her brow.

Connell tugged that distracting scrap free and teased the tip of it over her nose. She giggled and grabbed it from his fingers. "I don't want to fall in love," he said, leaning back in his chair.

Constance swatted at him with her ribbon. "But if you *did*."

He shook his head. "I decidedly don't."

She tapped her foot in annoyance. He was being deliberately obtuse and difficult. "Let us say there *was* a someone who was… attempting to give advice to, let's say, another young lady about what it would take to earn not your affections, but the affections of someone like you. What advice might you give?"

"I'd say don't bother, because the gent probably isn't interested," he said, his expression deadpan.

She pounced, sticking a finger in the air. "Aha! *Probably* isn't." That was altogether different than…

"*Definitely* isn't," he corrected, quashing that fledgling hope.

But he'd said it, and as such, she didn't intend to abandon him, or her intentions for him, anytime soon.

"Not love, then." She would allow him that concession. "But more of what you shared the other day." More specifically, she yearned for a day before that one, when he'd taken her in his arms and showed her more passion than she'd known in the whole of her thirty years.

He perked up. "You wish to dance the mazurka again?"

Yes. "No." She'd longed for it since the moment she'd fled his household.

Then she caught the little glimmer in his eyes.

The scoundrel…

Constance pursed her mouth, refusing to give him the satisfaction of knowing he'd riled her. Or worse, have him look too close to see that, if he asked her to follow him to that ballroom, she'd suggest they mazurka themselves all the way there. "What is another way a lady might snag your"—he gave her a look—"er… *attention*," she substituted in place of *heart*.

"Life pool," he said almost instantly.

"Life pool?" she echoed. "What in blazes is that?"

The hard slash of his lips pulled up at one corner. That devastating rogue's half grin played mayhem with her senses. "It is a form of pocket billiards."

She struggled to hold on to his explanation, her gaze riveted on his mouth, that same mouth that had been upon hers. *You yearn for that same kiss even now,* a silent voice jeered. "I've never heard of it," she made herself say. *So this is why ladies lose their wits for a scoundrel.* And here she'd believed that being a mature woman of thirty, she would be immune to that charm.

"It's not very much different from traditional billiards. In fact, I find it *almost* as intoxicating as watching a young lady indulge in spirits."

If he thought to shock her, he was to be greatly disappointed. "You refer to the previous and scandalous company you kept."

His lips formed another wicked smile. "Actually, I wasn't."

It took a moment for his words to register. When they did, her breath lodged in her lungs. He couldn't be talking about her. And yet, his meaning was there behind thick, golden lashes that he'd hooded. She wasn't a young lady and hadn't been for many years. No one, however, would ever be immune to him or his rogue's charms.

To give her trembling fingers something to do, she jotted down nonsensical notes.

He turned a question on her. "Do you play?"

"M-me?"

"You're the only guest I have present." And according to his vociferous servants, the only company he'd had in a very long time. Her heart tugged for altogether different reasons.

"I... haven't in years," she finally allowed. "My brother taught me, but my father never played, and so after my brother left..." And after the debts had become insurmountable, they had sold off every last article in the billiards room. "I never played again," she finished.

Her face burned from the heated intensity of his searching gaze.

Then the legs of his chair scraped along the floor.

Constance was already shaking her head. "Absolutely not," she said the moment he unfurled his tall, lithe frame.

"I haven't even said anything, love."

Love. There it was again. A casual endearment that, when spoken in his low, smooth baritone, had a quixotic effect on her senses.

Constance looked on helplessly as he came around the desk. She curled her toes into the old buckled shoes she'd commandeered from her mother's wardrobe. "I'm not joining you for a game of billiards, Connell." As it was, skating and dancing and drinking with him had proven perilous to the preservation of her heart.

"We're not playing billiards."

Some of the tension left her.

He grinned. "We're playing *life pool.*"

It was a struggle enough keeping her wits about her when they were exchanging words, but to engage in any more of the pastimes he found pleasure in? The same activities she herself did? She couldn't. There'd already been too many shared passions. *But it will be the last time you see him. The last lesson he provides.* She wavered, but then found her footing. "I'm not."

He scoffed. "*Of course* you are." Connell began gathering up her things. "A woman who indulges in spirits, visits me without the benefit of a chaperone, and issues advice to young ladies is hardly one to shrink over a game of billiards."

Only, it wasn't just that game of billiards. Why, she'd nearly not recovered from their dancing. And yet, she couldn't confess as much. Not when doing so would reveal she was weak around him. Weak, when she'd never been weak before any man.

Constance made one last attempt. "I don't see how playing billiards with you offers me anything more than simply speaking on it."

He lifted an eyebrow. "Ah, but that is the lesson, then, isn't it?"

She faltered.

In so many ways.

In every way.

In the intensification of this hungering to join him.

In her fear of what joining him would ultimately mean.

Connell shook his fingers. "Well?"

He might as well have been Lucifer with an apple in hand, and blast if she didn't know why Eve had made the whole of every person thereafter pay the price.

Bloody hell.

She was lost.

Snatching her bag back, Constance ignored his hand and hopped to her feet. "Let's get on with it," she gritted out.

He flashed a triumphant smile and led the way.

Fortunately, he didn't speak any further or issue additional endearments. That brief, much-needed reprieve allowed her to collect her wits and organize her thoughts.

Until they entered the billiards room...

Not breaking stride, he made for the cue rack between the floor-to-ceiling windows that framed the back of his residence… and shrugged out of his jacket.

The bag slipped from her fingers, landing with a loud *thwack* upon the limewashed hardwood floors. "Wh-what are you *doing*?" she croaked.

He tossed a glance over one of his broad shoulders. "Gathering the cue sticks," he said. Be it a deliberate or not misunderstanding, she was grateful.

Connell tossed his jacket, and all the muscles of his back rippled from that slight movement.

The black tailcoat landed along the back of a crimson-upholstered provincial armchair.

Constance exhaled slowly through her lips.

She'd not survive this.

Connell, the Duke of Renaud, in nothing more than shirt-sleeves had been dangerous before. After their kiss? Seeing him in any state of dishabille only tempted her with imaginings of experiences she'd never thought to know. Passion. Lovemaking.

"Given you're familiar with billiards, I trust you won't find this altogether different." He spoke like an instructor schooling his student, and to see him in any light different than perfectly masculine and virile made it far easier to think. He removed first one and then a second cue from the wall and came forward.

Retrieving her bag from where it had lain forgotten at her feet, she shook her head. "I don't need to play. I *do* need to take notes."

Which wasn't untrue. The whole purpose in her being here, in having sought him out, was to secure information for Mrs. Matcher's advice column.

"If you wish to school ladies on how to win the affections—"

"*The heart.*"

"—of a duke," he continued over that interposition, "do be sure to advise them that they need not just know what pastimes to take part in, but that they actually do take part."

"Given I'm not trying to win your affections," she said dryly, "I'll be sure to include that bit of guidance in my column."

"My heart."

She cocked her head.

"I do believe what you intended to say is that you're not trying to win *my heart*. If there was, of course, a heart to win." He followed that cynical quip with a little wink.

Constance attempted to come up with a suitably flippant reply… and failed.

Connell rested one cue against the side of the table, and with the other in hand, he walked about the table, eyeing the colored balls at the center. All the while, she watched him.

Only, his wasn't merely *a walk*. Walking was casual. Mere mortals did it. But there was nothing pedestrian about his steps. Or, really, any part of the gentleman.

His steps were sleek and provocative, each move accentuating the hard contours of thighs that other gentlemen did not possess. That knowledge came from staring out at countless men partnering other ladies on ballroom floors. No, not a single one bore the physique of Connell Wordsworth.

Constance's mouth went dry.

"It really is rather deficient, you know."

There is nothing deficient about him.

Connell stopped on the opposite end of the table so that they faced each other, and he gave her an odd look. "There's nothing deficient about *whom*?"

Whom?

Then it hit her—she'd spoken aloud.

"You," she blurted.

Both his eyebrows went arcing up.

Constance's entire body burst with a different heat. She felt the mortification paint her cheeks red. "Uh… that is, there is nothing deficient about your *billiards skills*," she recovered and resisted the urge to give a pleased toss of her head.

He gave a perfectly ducal lift of his head. "Thank you." Connell smiled. "Considering I've not taken my first shot yet, I appreciate that good faith in my abilities." Repositioning his stick, he set the cue flying. The end scraped the velvet lining. His ball jumped and then rolled idly into the other balls. They barely moved.

Constance stared on, horrified. "It appears I stand corrected in terms of my faith in your billiards skills."

"Given we're speaking of deficiencies, I should clarify that I was referring to your Mrs. Matcher's."

She bristled. "I beg your pardon?"

"It's just, you're providing guidance to ladies on a game—life pool—that you don't even know how to play."

"First"—she lifted a finger—"I'm not offering up advice on billiards." Constance put up another digit. "Second, if we're being fair, based on your break, you don't know much about playing, Connell."

"Ah, perhaps not." He pointed the end of his cue her way. "But I never professed to be a master at playing. Just that I enjoy doing so and that I'd hope any lady I spent forever with would feel the same." Connell resumed playing, leaving her with only the echo of his words for company.

He'd painted an image so very real: of him and a happy wife in a joyous union where husband and wife shared in each other's lives. Not the separation that existed amongst the *ton*, where even when there was affection between spouses, there often weren't shared interests.

And she found herself eaten slowly inside by envy for the woman who'd find that future with him.

She went absolutely motionless. Nay. She'd not meant *with* him. But rather, the manner of happy marriage he'd spoken of. He was the last man she should ever want or desire… in any way. Yes, she'd melted in his arms one time, but that physical response? It was vastly different than ponderances of more… with him.

Guilt ate at her.

For, every favorable thought, every longing she had of Connell was a betrayal. She shouldn't be enjoying her time here with him. Yes, Emilia was the manner of woman who'd understand that Constance had been driven to help by a letter written by a little girl.

But would she understand Constance falling under the duke's spell?

Never.

How could Emilia understand it when Constance didn't even

understand it herself?

As long as she kept their relationship clinical, purpose-driven—with her helping him and him helping her—then all would be fine.

Connell took another shot.

She winced as his ball sailed past all the balls still nestled near the center of the velvet table.

Constance whipped open her notebook.

His billiards skills mattered not.

Or rather, his lack of them.

She made a note and peeked over. Connell had his back to her once more. He leaned his weight over the table, practicing the back-and-forward thrust of his cue before taking his shot.

Crack.

Well, that shot hadn't been entirely terrible. This time, he'd at least managed to hit something. Other than the gorgeous velvet tabling, that was.

Oh, God, it was just too much. She couldn't do this.

"Your grip and bridge technique are atrocious." The words burst from her as he leaned over the table to yet again wound his poor table.

Turning slowly back, he faced her. "Excuse me?"

Constance dropped her notebook and pencil upon a nearby gilded chair. "Your grip and bridge," she said again as she joined Connell. She took the cue from him. "The bridge hand is vital to a player's success. It must provide a stable place for the cue to travel. Like this." Settling herself at the edge of the table, she positioned the cue and demonstrated the correct technique. "See how I've balanced my weight?"

"I… do." His harsh, guttural acknowledgment brought her attention briefly back to him.

The heat in his gaze burned. It burned in the most beautiful and perilous way. The heat was gone so quickly, she might have imagined that momentary flash of wickedness. "Now you," she said, abruptly straightening. Constance returned his cue.

As he shifted his weight forward, she assessed him, focusing on his technique and not on the way the elegant wool trousers pulled and strained across his thighs. Or she tried not to.

"Don't lean your support here. Your stance needs to carry your weight."

"Like this?" he quizzed, tossing her a glance.

She nodded jerkily. His legs braced as they were only further displayed those massive, tree-trunk-size legs. Her heart thumped wildly. "Yes," she said when he gave her another look. "Like that." Just like… *that*.

Any woman would be hard-pressed not to admire a man with his muscled physique. In fact, one might argue it would be unnatural if she didn't take a moment to appreciate the beauty of the man's human form.

Focus.

"As for your hand," she murmured, "relax it." She brushed her fingers over his before she thought better of it, before she could call that touch back. And yet, selfishly, she didn't want to. "Don't rest it on the table. Not to form a bridge. Raised, as you've been doing, makes your hand and position unstable. As you had it before," she guided him back into that erroneous positioning, "required you to elevate the back end of your cue. However, contact with the ball is best when the cue is as level to the table as possible." Constance returned his long fingers to the correct hold.

Together, they arched forward, his body perfectly angled and hers behind.

Constance's body temperature ticked up several degrees, and she closed her eyes against the onslaught of feeling. Who would have imagined that billiards could be so erotic?

When she opened her eyes, she found Connell's gaze again on her, an unfathomable expression in those deep-blue eyes.

"Wh-what is it?" she asked.

"I was correct," he said in quiet tones. "Billiards is surely the way to any duke's heart."

The air hissed and popped like the earth right before a lightning strike.

Her breathing increased.

Their fingers twined, wrapping around and between like climbing ivy. Feeling very much like she was ensnared by that tenacious green, she could not bring herself to break the contact. She reveled in the forbidden tingles that burned a path up her arm.

Then Connell tugged her forward into his arms, and she went. She went gladly and eagerly and with abandon.

He lowered his mouth to hers, but she was already up on tiptoe, meeting his lips in an explosion of passion.

Only, where last time there'd been heat, today there was fire. And it burned her up from the inside, a conflagration she was all too happy to perish in.

Connell licked at the seam of her lips, teasing them open, and she welcomed the fiery lash of his flesh against hers. His tongue was a brand that set her to further melting.

Constance's legs went weak, and he filled his hands with her buttocks and guided her atop the side of the billiards table. She let her legs splay open, wanting him close. Needing him closer. "Connell," she begged against his mouth. Clutching at the front of his shirt, she dragged him closer.

Only, it wasn't enough.

"You are magnificent," he panted between kisses.

Magnificent. Her whole life, she'd only ever been viewed or treated as so very ordinary in every way. And that praise only further emboldened her.

Angling her head, she deepened their kiss.

Distantly, she registered his fingers catching her ancient hem and dragging her skirts up. Up. Even higher up. Her thin stockings proved little barrier to the cool that kissed at her skin.

With an infinite slowness that threatened to drive her mad, he rolled her silk stockings down. Her breath caught on a broken gasp. "C-Connell." It was a plea for more, when everything inside her said, *End this, walk away, maintain your honor.* And yet, she was weak in every way. For she was no more capable of shattering this moment in his arms than she was of severing a limb.

"What is it?" he teased on a husky whisper.

Then he dropped to his knees and caught her ankle in his hand. Constance's eyes slid shut.

"I…" His lips teased a path along that inseam where her foot met her lower leg. He flicked the tip of his tongue along that sensitive spot. "I... ahhhh..." Her forgotten question or response, all jumbled in her mind now, was lost to a keening moan.

Constance dug her hands into the table, and her fingernails sank ever so slightly into that hard wood. It was just her foot. How was it possible that such a simple act upon such a casual part could elicit such a frenzied hungering inside?

As if he'd followed her thoughts, Connell paused his torturous exploration to glance up. "You were saying?" That graveled whisper teased her skin.

Constance bit her lip hard, and she shook her head. Had there been a question? Had she spoken? It was impossible. Not when she was incapable of anything but feeling.

Connell returned his attentions to her exposed legs. She panted, each rapid intake straining the vise about her lungs as she waited. Frozen. Half fearing what would come next. More agonized by the thought of what would not come.

He left a trail of kisses, alternately licking a path up her thigh and pressing his lips to that heated flesh.

Connell lifted her heavy skirts up about her waist. Balanced on the table as she was, she was left open and exposed before him...

CHAPTER 14

CONSTANCE BRANDLEY DIDN'T WEAR UNDERGARMENTS.

She wasn't the first woman he'd bedded who'd not bothered with those articles, but she was the first innocent he'd ever sought to give pleasure to.

And there was something so very heady, so very erotic in that tangle of damp, blonde curls. His vision unimpeded, he was able to worship with his gaze… and more.

Constance stiffened, and he knew the precise instant she was about to pull away.

Connell rested his palms on the insides of her creamy, white thighs. "You're beautiful."

Tension marred the mouth that had just moments ago been slack with passion. "I trust you find it scandalous."

"Yes," he allowed, and she made to shimmy down. "But scandalous isn't a sin. Not in this instance. And in this moment." Gathering her foot, he raised her leg slowly, allowing her to withdraw should she truly wish to. But she didn't. He stopped, his lips nearly brushing against her calf. "I find"—*you*—"it absolutely entrancing."

Passion stirred again in her eyes, and she relaxed her hips.

Cupping his hands around her waist, he drew her nearer his mouth.

Constance's breath hitched as her body unwittingly shifted closer to the edge of the table, bringing her closer to the edge of reason.

The scent of her—woman and musk and the hint of rose water—clogged his senses.

He dropped a kiss atop her mound, and her hips came shooting up. Her fists clenched the edge of the table, and by the white-knuckled grip she had, she'd leave marks upon that wood, and he'd forever visit this room, remembering her and this... and them together.

"I—I don't suppose I sh-should mention this in Mrs. Matcher's?"

For the first time ever in the midst of lovemaking, Connell laughed.

"Wh-what i-is it?" The breathless quality of her voice ruined any hint of affront.

He pressed a kiss against the satiny soft flesh of the inside of her thigh. "Constance Brandley, if you are teasing in this moment, I'm doing something very, *very* wrong."

Constance tangled her fingers in his hair and anchored him close. "O-oh," she panted. "Qu-quite the opposite. You are d-doing everything v-very, v-very right."

He chuckled, his body shaking from desire and amusement.

"In f-fact, I'd be w-wisssse—" Her breath hissed between her lips as he dragged his tongue over her slit. Connell worked his mouth over her, teasing her folds, suckling them until Constance was incoherent, crying out his name and moaning in between.

"What was that?" He ceased his ministrations and teased.

She whimpered. "*Connell*," she implored and scolded, both at the same time.

He flicked his tongue at that sensitive nub. "You were saying?"

"I'd be wise to wr-write about th-thisssss." A cry exploded from her as he lapped her.

His body throbbed and ached from the need to make love to her. He found himself swept up in an explosive wave of passion, the kind that distracted, that made a man forget his name. Or right from wrong. Bringing a respectable lady to pleasure on his billiards table, surely fit in the "wrong" column.

He'd never been one for rules or respectability, though.

Connell slid his hands under her buttocks, bringing her ever closer to his mouth. Constance's hips took on a frantic rhythm as she lifted and thrust, undulating wildly.

He groaned. Or he thought it was him. Lust left a haze over reason.

Connell slipped a finger into her sheath, and she cursed, tightening her legs about his head. All the while, she keened and moaned her pleasure. And he thrilled in those bold, beautiful sounds of her desire.

It was too much. He yanked his shirt off and let it fall to the floor, and then he freed himself from his breeches. His shaft sprang forward, aching and hard.

Constance's lashes fluttered open, as if they were heavy and the task difficult.

Her red lips, still swollen from their earlier kiss, parted.

He stopped. He ached and burned, but wanted this decision to be hers.

Then she stretched her fingers out.

A hiss slipped from him as she took him in her hand, as bold as she'd been through their every exchange.

"It's quite hard and soft like satin, both at the same time," she noted in breathless tones, as matter-of-fact as she would be recording notes for her Mrs. Matcher's column.

Connell closed his eyes and struggled to retain control through her ministrations. She moved her hand over him.

It was too much.

Climbing onto the pool table, he guided Constance into the middle so that she was stretched under him. He again found her with his fingers. Her channel was sopping wet.

She moaned, and he swallowed that delectable sound with his kiss. They tangled with their tongues. They stroked each other. Their mouths moved as perfectly as their bodies. As perfectly as they did with their every encounter.

Connell positioned himself between her legs and paused. Sweat collected at his brow.

His and Constance's gazes locked. Her eyes radiated all the desire and passion wreaking havoc on him and rational thought. But he left the ultimate decision to her. If she wanted to end this now, he would. It would take a Herculean effort, and his body would be left with this agonizing ache, but he'd not make love to her unless this was what she truly wanted.

Then she tangled her fingers in his hair and brought his head down so their lips could meet once more, and he had her answer.

Connell again found the moist tangle of curls between her legs, and he worked another finger and then another inside of her, until she was crying out, incoherent. Moving his fingers, he pressed himself against her and slid slowly inside her tight sheath, even as his body screamed out to take her.

Constance slipped her hands up his chest and scraped her nails lightly over his skin. "Don't you dare stop," she ordered, and it was a command of the gods.

He thrust home in a smooth, fluid stroke.

She briefly stiffened, but then she lifted her hips again in that desperate up-and-down rhythm. Inviting him to move.

And he moved. Slow, teasing strokes designed to torture her. To drag every vestige of agonizing pleasure from her. "Please," she begged.

"How does it feel?"

She bit her lower lip. "S-so good. So very. Verrry… ahh…" she cried out as he thrust deeper. "Good."

Connell quickened his thrusts, pushing her higher and further. Closer.

Outside, the wind howled and battered at the windows, lending a frenzy to the moment.

He felt the walls of her closing about him and knew before her lips even parted on the scream that rent the room.

"*Connellllll.*" Constance came undone in his arms, and he continued to plunge himself deep inside her.

When she'd gone limp under him, he pulled out and spilled himself along the inside of her thigh. Gasping for breath, Connell collapsed, catching himself at his elbows to keep from crushing her.

He rolled onto his side, and with his chest heaving, he stared at the crystal chandelier affixed directly overhead. And as Connell's heart resumed a normal rhythm, he registered one detail:

He'd made love to Constance Brandley upon a billiards table.

When she'd deserved a bed and far more than… a scoundrel such as him.

Scoundrel that he was, he couldn't bring himself to regret the act. Oh, he wished there'd been more than this for her first time, but he'd not change this moment. Not for…

Constance's body tensed, shattering those musings.

His stomach fell.

By the white of her face, she was, however, of an altogether different mind frame. "Constance—"

"This shouldn't have happened," she whispered, and she might as well have thrust a spear into his chest. She sat abruptly up.

"I'm sor—"

She frantically shook her head. "No, it's my fault. I wanted this. I wanted *you*."

He preened inside. Lightness suffused his chest.

Except… there was no joy in her tone. Only regret.

How was it possible for *I wanted you* to have been uttered like it was a sin and a shame? Unable to look at her, he edged over on the table and reached for his shirt below. His fingers brushed—and he leaned… too far.

Connell tumbled onto the floor, falling… as hard as he had for the woman who now peered down at him.

"Connell? Are you—?"

"Fine," he lied. He wasn't fine in this moment, and he was never going to be fine again. For he, who'd vowed to never let anyone in, had gone and tumbled hopelessly and helplessly head over heels for this woman. Gathering up his shirt, he stood and gently cleaned the remnants of his seed from her body.

All the while, he felt her gaze on him.

When he'd finished, he helped right her garments… and her hair.

They were acts he'd performed so many times before with too many different women. But never once had what preceded it been about anything more than a physical act. A momentary gratification, and hearts had certainly never been engaged.

Not as his was in this instant, with Constance Brandley.

"Marry me?" he blurted.

It was harder to say who was more startled by that question.

Her or him.

What was worse, was the horror that filled her expressive eyes, those crystalline windows into her soul. "Is that an offer or a question?"

His heart thumped. What was he thinking? Marriage? He didn't want anyone in his life. Not like this. Did he? Either way, having made love to her, a respectable lady, it was only the right decision. "Both?"

A panicky little laugh escaped her. "Oh, Connell…"

Oh, Connell. They were surely the two words and tone that had begun every last rejection any lady had ever given any man.

"You don't even want anyone in your life. And me?" Constance waved her hands down her person. "I'm the last person…"

Because of Emilia…

Emilia, the woman he'd been betrothed to and cared for, but whom he'd never truly known… or loved. Not like this. He'd been a boy with a fanciful idea of what love was. But there'd been no shared connection. Because he'd been too much a boy to even know what that was.

He watched blankly as Constance rushed to gather up her things. So that she could leave… and he'd never again see her.

He'd done his gentlemanly duty. He'd asked, she'd all but declined, and as such, he should be relieved for it. So why wasn't he? Why, instead, was there this boulderlike weight crushing his chest and making it hard to get air into his lungs?

He tried once more. "You were a virgin."

Constance donned her cloak and drew her satchel over her arm. "I'm a thirty-year-old woman. Not a debutante and not a young marriage-minded miss. I'm capable of my own decisions."

This was it, then. The end of their time together.

Constance stopped before him.

Say something, he silently urged himself.

She wet her lips. "Thank you… for everything. I shall miss our meetings."

He'd miss her and their meetings.

He caught her fingers in his, and she stared at their linked digits. "Goodbye, Constance," he said quietly.

She made for the door and then stopped at that panel, looking as though she wished to say something more.

But she didn't.

An instant later, she was gone.

And at last, Connell had that which he'd believed he wanted—to be alone.

Only to discover, with Constance gone and out of his life, how very wrong he'd been.

CHAPTER 15

One week later

HE HAD NO RIGHT TO be here.

Though, in fairness, there wasn't really a place Connell belonged.

He was a man, lost.

Mayhap he'd always been.

Only, a short while ago, he'd let his misery consume him. He'd been content to wallow in his own anger and frustration and bitterness. He wasn't that man any longer.

Oh, he'd always be lonely and wish there was more, the life he'd imagined for himself, with a family. But he had joyous memories to keep with him. Moments filled with such happiness and laughter, gifts to be cherished and not spat upon with resentment for a selfish hungering for more.

Constance had shown him that.

She'd made him stop and think about just how very fortunate he'd been and how wrong it was to not look joyfully back at those times he had been given. With Iris. With Hazel.

Even if those moments had been shorter than he'd anticipated or yearned for, it was still a time that had been.

And Constance.

For, if he was being truthful with himself, which he'd become abundantly so since she'd entered his life and challenged him to it, he missed her. And this great, gaping hole that had taken root in the place where his heart should be had been there since her parting.

It didn't matter that it had been only a short while since she'd first stepped through his townhouse doors. She'd reminded him of what it was to laugh again and smile and think… and want to live again.

You don't even want anyone in your life. And me?

"How wrong I was," he finally answered her, only now, into the quiet of the Leeds nighttime sky. The response had come too late, because he'd not known until she'd walked away just how wrong he'd been.

Wind howled and whipped his cloak about his legs as he stared down the narrow drive to the modest cottage. The room, awash with light from a fire's glow, illuminated the cheerful tableau playing out behind the lead windowpanes: a mother, a father, and a daughter, all sitting about while the father read and the pair with him looked adoringly up.

I should leave.

I should never have come.

Connell glanced briefly at his mount tied to a riding block at the end of the short drive, reconsidering the decision to come here. When he looked back, it was to find a face pressed against the lightly frosted windowpane.

Iris' breath had warmed the glass, and she rubbed a circle in it until her line of vision to Connell was unimpeded.

The moon's glow bore down, illuminating the joy in the little girl's expression. She waved frantically.

How he'd missed her. Emotion stuck in his throat, and he lifted his hand, returning her greeting.

But she'd already looked behind her. Her excited shouts came muffled, but still vivid.

As Hazel and her new husband opened the door, Iris went flying past them. Her little boots kicked up gravel and rocks as she went. Lengthening his strides, Connell hurried to meet the little girl who'd been like a daughter to him.

"Hullo, pop—oomph." His greeting ended on a grunt as she launched herself at him.

"Uncle *Connellll*," she cried happily, wrapping her arms about his waist.

He hefted her into his arms and cradled her close. "Poppet," he whispered against her ear.

"You came!" she piped in, edging back so she might see his face. "I'm so glad you did. I have so much to tell you. It snowed, Uncle Connell. *Snowwwwed.*" Her little nose wrinkled. "There's none anymore, but there was, and my papa took me out, and we played snowballs and ice skated and…" She chattered on, as she'd always done, and there was such a familiarity to it. As though they'd never been apart. As though he'd bothered to send a note or respond to her letters.

What a bastard he'd been. He was undeserving of her devotion.

When there was a break in discourse, he set her down. "Come along. You're going to catch a chill." She slid her hand into one of his and tugged him the remaining length of the walk.

Hazel greeted him with a wide smile. A late cousin's daughter, she'd been a girl of just seventeen when he'd first met her. Now, she was a more mature version of the broken-hearted ward he'd taken in. "Connell." Stepping aside so that he might enter, Hazel stretched her palms out. "How very lovely it is to see you."

It didn't escape his notice that her husband, Mr. Landry, hovered close at her shoulder, lingering there as if he feared Connell had come to take those he loved. And once, Connell would have wanted to do just that. The trio, though? They were happy, and he appreciated that the love and joy they knew together was more than the selfish desire he'd had to keep them in his life.

"Would you care for a coffee or tea?" she asked as Connell shrugged out of his cloak, and her husband shut the door behind them.

Small but cozy and toasty and warm, there was nothing more any family could possibly need or want. "No. No refreshments are necessary."

He hovered.

Except, now that he'd come and intruded, he didn't know what to say.

A look passed between husband and wife. Some unspoken communication and language that Connell had no understanding of… but had briefly known with another.

Constance.

"Coffee for His Grace," Hazel directed her husband as she retrieved the cloak draped over Connell's arm and hung it on a hook behind the door.

"That won't be necessary," Connell called after the younger man.

"Hush," she chided and motioned to her husband, and the other man rushed off.

Connell stared on wistfully. In command and decisive, Hazel bore little resemblance to the young girl he'd at first resented.

"Sit."

"You are happy, I trust?" he asked after he'd settled onto the old upholstered sofa, and Hazel scrambled onto the seat beside him. Because if she or her daughter were anything other than overjoyed, he'd see Landry destroyed. Except, mother's and daughter's easy smiles and soft features were all the confirmation Connell needed.

"We are well."

They proceeded to regale Connell with all they'd been up to since they'd last seen one another. When they finished, there was a brief moment of awkwardness.

"I came to apologize," he said gruffly. He tugged his gloves off and slapped the leather articles together distractedly. "I've… shut you both out, and it was petty and wrong, and… I'd ask that you please allow me another chance to be part of your lives."

Giggling, Iris pinched him. "That is silly, Uncle Connell. Of course we want you in our lives. Isn't that right, Mama?"

His ward held a hand out toward her daughter, and Iris joined her, sliding her fingers into hers. "Of course we do. You have done nothing but give where Iris and I are concerned. You opened your home and your heart to us, and you will always be our family. There is nothing to forgive," she said simply, and another wave of emotion assaulted him.

He briefly closed his eyes. "Thank you."

"What has accounted for the change?" Hazel asked curiously.

There was only one person responsible for any good he'd found—Constance. "I may have met someone who helped me to see that I've been a miserable bas… uh…" He clawed at his collar.

Iris giggled. "You were going to say bastard, weren't you?"

Her mother gave her a sharp look.

"I may have been," Connell allowed with a wink. He cleared his throat. "Either way, I've realized I've been incredibly selfish, thinking first of my own hurts, when what has mattered most is that you both are happy."

Tears lit Hazel's eyes. "We are. I never wanted to see you hurt." Pulling a kerchief from her apron, she dabbed at her eyes. "Who is she?"

Who is she?

Was.

Constance existed in the past; the near one, but the memory of her was still as fresh as if they'd had one of their lessons yesterday morn. "Just… someone I know."

A little twinkle glimmered in Iris' gaze. "It is Mrs. Matcher, isn't it?" she asked eagerly.

"Clever girl," he muttered, rubbing the top of her head.

"What…?" His former ward glanced perplexedly between Connell and her daughter. "Who?"

"I wrote a letter to Mrs. Matcher and asked her to help Uncle Connell be happy again. And she did. It's the only thing that makes sense." She hopped up and down. "Have you met her? I love her column so very much."

"I have," he said hoarsely. "And I… like her very much."

Nay, he didn't just *like* Constance Brandley… he loved her. He loved her so very much.

Where there would have been horror and fear at that realization, there was now only a wistful sadness.

Mother and daughter peered at him with gazes entirely too wise and mature for their years. "You care for her, don't you?" Hazel murmured.

He started.

His former ward pointed her eyes at the ceiling. "Of course I can see that. You needn't just say it for us to know how you are feeling."

Connell chuckled, the sound rusty to his own ears. "She invaded my household… at Iris' urging, and she changed my life."

Iris jumped up. "You're in love! You're in *lovvvve,*" she cried happily, spinning herself in a little circle. She abruptly stopped, and her lips tilted down. "Why aren't you smiling if you're in love with Mrs. Matcher?"

"Because… it's complicated." There was the matter of her loyalty to Emilia and…

Iris tugged at his hand. "Have you told her how you feel?"

He opened his mouth and then closed it. His brow furrowed. He hadn't. Not that it would necessarily alter her feelings either way, nor change anything. And yet…

His heart hammered. "I didn't."

Iris rolled her eyes. "Uncle Connnnelll, a woman won't be with a man who doesn't have the courage to tell her he loves her."

She was right. Perhaps there'd be no future between him and Constance, and all he'd have left were the all-too-brief memories they'd shared. But neither had he made her a real offer of marriage. She'd believed his question had been motivated by honor, which it had been. Or at least as he'd presented it.

Catching Iris, he drew her close for a hug, ringing a little laugh from her. "You're right," he whispered.

She winked. "Of course I am."

He jumped up. "I have to go to her."

"Yes, you do," Hazel agreed. Coming to her feet, she took his hand. "However, you'll need to warm up, have a meal, and exchange your mount before you go."

A short while later, with his ward and her husband and little Iris waving after him, Connell went galloping back to London.

CHAPTER 16

HER COLUMN WAS COMPLETE.

It was time to relinquish control of Mrs. Matcher's back to Emilia.

She'd written column after column of mostly mediocre advice and had earned herself coin. Not enough to see her cello returned, but enough to find pride in even those small earnings.

She should be besieged only by joy.

And she *wanted* to cry.

Only, hers were not tears of happiness.

She wanted to weep for so many reasons: because she'd enjoyed Mrs. Matcher's. Because she'd enjoyed working on it with Connell. Because today was the day she'd return those responsibilities to her friend, the friend she'd betrayed in every way.

Constance wanted to cry all the harder for that betrayal. For, what was worse, she couldn't bring herself to feel the proper guilt she should. Because, selfishly, she loved Connell more.

When he'd offered her marriage, that false, empty offer born of a gentleman's honor, all she'd wanted was to give him a yes and live out a life of performing the mazurka and ice skating and playing life pool…

Tears threatened, those drops filling her eyes and blurring the words of the recently completely pages. She blinked them back.

"Life p-pool," she whispered. She'd never again look upon a billiards table without thinking of him awakening her body to desire and bringing her to the greatest pleasure she'd ever known.

And what did that say about Constance as a friend? What did

it say that her greatest regrets came in missing him and the time they'd shared together and not in the betrayal she'd carried out these past weeks, with her actions, with her thoughts, and worse, with her yearnings?

Footfalls echoed from the hall, and without bothering to knock, Scott drew the door open. For a moment where hope was born, she thought it was him. "Oh," she blurted as Scott introduced the marchioness.

And there was a keen disappointment.

"That is hardly the greeting a best friend should ever hope to receive," Emilia drawled as Scott retreated and shut the door behind him.

"Emilia," she said to the first and closest friend she'd ever had. "What are you doing here?" Before Emilia could answer, she added, "You shouldn't be here." It was as though guilt had conjured her.

"I wanted to see you," the other woman said. Guilt pitted in Constance's belly as her friend ambled over and settled into the seat beside Constance's. "I'll not be one of those women who retires to the countryside to do nothing more than wait."

And yet, flouting those conventions as Emilia did, she'd still forsaken her work as Mrs. Matcher these past months.

Then the truth hit Constance all at once. She sank onto the edge of her chair. "You only did it because of me," she said softly. "Because of my circumstances." That was the only reason a headstrong, capable woman such as Emilia would have relinquished those responsibilities.

Emilia scoffed. "Of course not." The other woman beamed. "We've helped one another."

The blade of guilt twisted all the more. How wrong her friend was. Constance had made a bumble of the other woman's advice column, and to boot, Constance had been paying visits to Emilia's former betrothed. And there was still the matter of Constance being head over heels in love with Connell Wordsworth, the Duke of Renaud.

Unable to meet Emilia's eyes, Constance attended the folder on her lap. To give her fingers something to do, she arranged and then rearranged the pages.

"Constance," Emilia began in a gentle voice, "I can't thank you enough for—"

"I can't do this," Constance blurted, interrupting the other woman in midsentence. She made herself look at her first and greatest friend in the world.

Flummoxed, her hands on her heavily rounded belly, Emilia opened and closed her mouth several times. "I don't... understand."

"I can't do this anymore. I can't write in your stead." It was a privilege she didn't deserve. "I'm so grateful that you've given me the opportunity to be Mrs. Matcher, and I know why you did it... to help me, and... and..." Constance thrust the folder into Emilia's hands and promptly dissolved into tears.

Struggling to get herself into a standing position, Emilia waddled over to Constance and lowered herself beside her. She folded an arm around Constance and hugged her close.

Constance wept all the harder. Burying her face in her hands, she shook from the fierceness of her tears. "I-I a-am the v-very worst o-of friends," she gasped between her sobs.

"Shh. Of course you're not," Emilia chided, stroking the back of Constance's head.

It was a devotion Constance was undeserving of.

"I-I am," she protested. Before her courage deserted her, she forced the words out. "I-I f-fell in l-love with him," she wept. Her ribs ached. Her whole body ached. And still that pain was welcome. "I-I didn't m-mean for it to h-happen, and I-I was l-loyal at f-first." But then she'd stepped through his door and joined him in his office, and absolutely everything had changed.

"You are... in love?" Puzzlement rang clear in Emilia's voice. "With... *who*?"

Oh, God. She had to say it, because of course it wouldn't be clear unless it was stated. Getting control of her tears and trembling, Constance forced her quavering hands to her lap. She folded them into one interlocked fist. "Connell."

Even through the sheen still blurring her eyes, Constance detected the confusion. "Connell?" her friend echoed. "As in..."

"The Duke of Renaud," Constance made herself finish when Emilia did not.

That admission ushered in a weighty silence.

Constance wiped at her eyes. "You hate me."

"Of course I don't hate you," her friend chastised, swatting her on the leg. "I'll allow I am… confused. You never even much liked Connell."

Because she sounded neither outraged, hurt, nor angry, Constance was able to continue. "I didn't really know him." Now she did, and she'd love him forever.

"And now you do?" Emilia ventured, without recrimination, her tone that of one still trying to work her way through a puzzle.

"Now I do." This time, she spoke more easily, starting from the only place that made sense—the beginning. "I received a letter one day." Reaching into the file, she withdrew the note she'd memorized from the outset and handed it over.

As Emilia took it and read, Constance continued.

When she finished with her telling, another round of silence met her. Constance was the one to fill it. "I didn't want to like him. I preferred to think of him as, and hate him for, being the scoundrel who broke your heart."

"He didn't really break my heart. Oh, at the time, I believed there was no greater pain than his ending our betrothal." A wistful smile danced on the edge of her lips. "But my heart wasn't even complete until Heath."

It was a statement Constance understood so very well. This love was unlike any she'd ever known. She sighed and rested against Emilia's side. "I fell in love with him, and I'm so sorry to you because of it, but I can't be sorry for loving him."

Emilia edged away and took her gently by the shoulders. "Do you truly believe I'm the manner of friend who'd begrudge you loving who you love?"

"But—"

"Yes, it is Connell. But I don't love him anymore. I do love you and know that your happiness is what matters to me, and I'd never resent your finding happiness with a man I thought I loved a lifetime ago."

A man she'd thought she loved…

Which implied she'd never truly loved him.

Constance wrapped her arms about Emilia and just clung tight to her. There was this great lifting, a weight moving from her shoulders and leaving only lightness in its place. And yet, she sucked in a shuddery sigh. That absolution from Emilia still did not bring with it Connell's love or anything at all with him, really.

"Now, may I read your latest column?" Emilia asked when they parted.

She nodded, and with knots twisting in her belly, she allowed her friend to open up that folder and read those pages.

Those lessons Constance had learned in five days, but would hold on to her forever.

She sat in silence while Emilia read, and when she'd closed the folder, she looked up.

"You hate it," Constance blurted.

Emilia made to speak.

"I just completed it this morn and believe I can make some revisions—"

"It is perfect, Constance. Just perfect." Emilia smiled, dimples forming in cheeks that were well-rounded from pregnancy. "Every last lady will be clamoring for the heart of a duke, and you've gone and equipped them with the very list they need to win one."

They shared a wistful smile as they were both brought back to the young girls they'd once been, searching for coin to purchase a Roma's magical pendant designed to win them the heart of a duke. If only there had been some magical amulet, after all.

"Thank you," Constance said softly.

Emilia shrugged. "We are friends." She pressed a hand to her belly. "This one is quite active, though, and I should return. Heath is in the carriage."

Constance popped up. "I'm so sorry. He—"

"Insists on joining me everywhere." Her eyes sparkled. "And it's really most sweet and welcome." She hesitated. "I want you to be happy. And I don't know if the Duke of Renaud is the man who can be the person to make you happy, but if he is, you only have my blessings."

Emotion stuck in her throat. "Thank you," she whispered, hugging her friend once more.

After she'd gone, Constance closed her eyes.

There was, if not happiness with Connell, peace in her friend's blessing.

Mayhap if you tell him how you feel. That you love him. Mayhap that might matter enough to make him forget about wanting to be alone.

Footsteps came from the hall once more. Scott's shuffling ones. Constance looked to the folder her friend had left behind. As the panel opened, Constance reached for the column. "I would have brought…" Her words faded into oblivion. Joy filled every corner of her.

A day's worth of growth marred his cheeks. His hair was tousled and his garments wrinkled. The faint hint of horseflesh clung to him, as if he'd been riding. And he'd never looked any more beautiful than he did in this instant. "*You.*"

Connell glanced about. "I… you were expecting another?" he said hesitantly as Scott, bless his devotion, backed out of the room, leaving them alone.

Had her heart ever been filled with this beautiful happiness?

She made herself nod. "Yes." He cocked his head. "No. I… that is… Emilia was here and left something behind."

He clasped his hands behind him and rocked forward on the balls of his feet. "I see."

She tried to make some sense of his response or his thoughts or any of what he was thinking or feeling. If the mention of Emilia meant anything, he gave no outward hint of it. And yet, he was here, with Constance, now.

Why?

And how very desperately she wanted the answer to be… for her.

"Would you like to sit?" she offered when they both remained standing in the middle of the parlor, unspeaking.

"Please." He made to take a step forward, but suddenly stopped. "You've been crying. Is everything all right?" he asked sharply, taking another step toward her.

Constance touched her cheeks. "Y-yes. I'm quite well." She let her hands fall to her sides.

Connell flattened his mouth, and she feared he'd press her, but he didn't. He let her to her lie.

He joined her at the chair beside the sofa, sitting near her, but not upon the same seat.

How stilted they were. Not even when they'd been cross with each other and mistrustful of the other's motives had there been this tension.

Constance folded her hands primly upon her lap.

"I wanted to thank you."

Her heart dropped. That was why he was here. "You already thanked me, Connell," she said, hoping he didn't hear the regret in that reminder. "You needn't—"

He shook his head. "I went to see my ward and her daughter, Hazel and Iris. They are happy, and"—he smiled—"I find that is enough."

That is enough…

And in a way, it was.

Constance lifted a hand to her chest, and perhaps it was true that love for another superseded all of one's own feelings, for learning he'd had closure and come to peace with those two people whom he so loved, mattered more in this moment than her selfish wish that she was the reason for his appearance.

Liar. You want him. You want all of him. And you want him to feel the same way about you.

"That isn't the only reason I've come," he murmured, and hope surged once more.

"Oh?" Her voice quivered.

Not taking his eyes from her face, Connell reached inside his jacket and withdrew a thick, official-looking packet.

She glanced down at the thick stack. "I don't…?" Confusion replaced that earlier emotion of hope as she accepted it at his silent urging.

"I can never repay you for the days we spent together, Constance. You brought me more joy, more hope than I've had in…" Connell edged closer so that their knees touched. Even through the fabric of her dress, her leg tingled with warmth. "Perhaps forever," he said softly. "You made me look at who I am and who I've been and helped me to see that I've not been the man I want to be. And I wanted to give you a gift you are deserving of." He nodded to the packet she held.

Looking at it, Constance slowly unfolded it and read the opening sentences of the top page.

She gasped. The stack fell noiselessly to her lap. And then she more than half feared that if she didn't retrieve it immediately, the words there would change. But they didn't. They remained there, in black ink, brought by Connell.

"I took the liberty of hiring a man to look into your brother's whereabouts. And that is what was discovered," he said solemnly. "I don't know the nature of his travels, but he's been moving about various parts of Europe. But he is well—"

Crushing those pages in her hands, Constance pressed them against her face. A sob escaped her.

He'd done this for her.

Connell had discovered the information her struggling family had gone even further into debt to seek. He'd used his own resources and surely his influence as a duke to find out about her only brother. She lowered her shaking hands. "Thank you," she said hoarsely. "I…"

He shook his head. "You don't want my thanks, and I don't want your thanks, either, Constance," he said simply. Connell shoved to his feet and, through the joy, came a curtain covering of fear that he'd leave.

She jumped up. "Please…" *Don't go. Stay, with me, always.*

"I've had eight hours in the saddle to prepare what I would say to you in this moment. And yet, Constance"—Connell turned his palms up—"I find myself without a single organized thought beyond just one." His gaze locked with hers. "How very much I've missed you…"

She clutched the beloved pages he'd just given her against her chest. "You… have?"

He drew in an unsteady breath. "Days were dark and my heart darker," he murmured in a low voice. "Every moment the same in my solitude. Until there was a knock… at the door. On my heart, and forevermore, I'd be altered. By my love for you. By my need for us to be joined in every way."

Constance caught her lower lip. "You wrote me a poem," she whispered.

"You know I'm horrid with them." He blushed, and she fell more madly, more deeply in love with him for that tender vulnerability. Connell dragged a hand through his hair. "I swore never to write one again and didn't think I'd be able to or want to, but you remind me what it is to laugh and love and live. And then one day, I just realized…"

Tears blurred her eyes. "Realized what?"

"Five days will never be enough, Constance Brandley. Not when I only want forever with you. I want to marry you," he blurted. "I want to spend forever with you and—"

On a sob, Constance hurled herself against him, knocking them off-balance and sending them careening onto the sofa. They bounced, the noisy springs squeaking. "I love you," she rasped.

His eyes lit. "You love me?"

Something between a cry and a laugh bubbled in her throat. She captured Connell's face between her hands. "You daft man. I love you and only you, and I want forever with you, Connell."

He grinned. "Then that is precisely what you shall have, my love."

Lowering her head, Constance took care to seal that promise… with a kiss.

EPILOGUE

Kent, England
Summer, 1823

THE WORLD AS CONSTANCE KNEW it was beginning.

It wasn't a flair for the dramatics that drove that understanding. Rather, it was the significance of what had taken place on this day.

Nor, for that matter, did Constance need Society's leading hostesses to point out it was bad form to miss one's wedding breakfast.

"We should be inside," Constance pointed out to the group of four women, outside in Connell's—and now Constance's—gardens.

"And whyever would you think that you, the bride, should be taking part in the bridal festivities?" Aldora drawled.

"Exactly," Emilia muttered. "No one will notice we've gone missing." With sweat on her brow, Emilia jammed the tip of her shovel into the ground, turning up another patch of earth.

Watching from the sidelines, Rowena laughed softly. "I believe Aldora was being facetious."

Aldora waggled her fingers. "She is correct. I was."

Huffing from her exertions, Emilia paused and wiped at her damp brow. "We've important matters to attend."

"More important than Constance's wedding day?" Meredith rejoined.

With the same pique reminiscent of many, many years earlier, when they'd been children arguing over a Roma woman's necklace, Emilia let her shovel fall and dropped her hands upon her hips. "We do. Very important matters. Why, we've children now. Babes. Some of us are expecting babes." She glanced pointedly at Meredith's and Rowena's rounded bellies. "And given everything we know of Renaud…"

Four pairs of eyes landed probingly on Constance. She felt her cheeks burning hot. "Oh, hush. We…" *Could be with child.* Her hands reflexively went to her belly. She and Connell had delayed the wedding so that Constance's brother could be found and notified and could return home for the joyous occasion. Also so that Emilia and Heath, the best friend Connell had found a new connection with, could also be present. Yes, they'd held off on marrying for several months, but she and Connell hadn't refrained from…

"By that blush on Constance's cheeks, it appears Emilia isn't far off with that supposition," Meredith drawled.

At her friends' laughter, Constance abruptly dropped her hands. "You're insufferable. The lot of you."

Rowena wrinkled her nose. "I will point out that I wasn't laughing."

"You were stifling a smile," Aldora piped in. "Which is very much the same thing."

"Is it?" Rowena shot back.

While a debate ensued, Constance found her gaze wandering the length of the gardens to the conservatory.

Her heart jumped.

At some point, another gathering had assembled.

"They are spying," Constance announced.

As one, each friend looked to the assembled gentlemen: two marquesses, two dukes, and a gentleman.

"Should I go tell them to leave?" Meredith offered, already starting down the graveled path.

Rowena sighed. "They aren't spying. Why, they aren't even paying us any notice."

Emilia went back to digging, and while Constance's friends continued chatting, she stared off in the distance to where Connell stood.

As Rowena had pointed out, the gentlemen were otherwise occupied. They gathered around Connell while he regaled them with some story or another, gesticulating as he spoke. Even with the space parting the groups, the rumbles of laughter carried. Whatever he said just then had Lord Heath doubled over with mirth.

A little sigh slipped out. Her husband could charm or regale anyone. That effortless ability had hopelessly ensnared her from the very moment she'd knocked on his door.

Her husband.

She rolled those words around in her mind, testing them. Hardly daring to believe that she'd not only married, but that she'd wed a man who'd captured her heart.

Just then, Connell glanced over.

Her heart jumped several beats.

Connell touched a hand to his chest. "I love you," he mouthed.

"I love you," she silently returned.

"I believe that should do it!" Emilia cried excitedly, shattering the moment and demanding Constance's attention.

And for the first time, she registered…

"That hole in my garden is rather large," Constance blurted. She took a step closer to the deep trench and peered inside.

Rowena ambled over until she stood shoulder to shoulder with Constance. "It is indeed deep."

"She's intending to bury someone," Meredith said in somber tones. "That is all there is to explain it."

Constance burst into laughter along with her friends.

Emilia scowled. "Oh, hush. You may be laughing now…" She paused to level a hard look at each of them. "But you won't be in eighteen years."

That managed to kill the mirth of Constance and the other women.

"This sounds all too familiar," Rowena muttered, eyeing the graveled path to where the gentlemen still laughed and mingled.

"Oh, no," Meredith said, gripping the other woman lightly by the forearm. "We are in this"—whatever the latest *this* Emilia had concocted for them—"together."

Emilia thumped the end of her shovel on the mound of soil she'd just unearthed. "I hear you."

"What in blazes are you up to now?" Aldora asked, folding her arms at her belly, lightly accentuating—

Constance flared her eyes.

"You are with child, too!" Emilia exclaimed. Her words emerged faintly accusatory.

A pink blush splotched Aldora's cheeks. "You needn't say it like *that*. Furthermore, I was going to tell you," the other woman grumbled.

Constance, Rowena, and Meredith surrounded the glowing mother-to-be. Or they attempted to.

Emilia clanged her shovel against a nearby wrought-iron statue. "There will be time enough for celebration after—"

"Does that also include Constance and Renaud's wedding festivities?" Aldora drawled. "Because it does seem essential to get back to all of that."

"We will," Emilia promised. "But first…" With a grand flourish, she fetched three satchels from behind a stone bench.

"Whenever did you have *those* delivered?" Constance mused.

"It is Emilia," Meredith pointed out. "She is capable of many great surprises."

"I may have had some assistance from Jennie. She's quite wonderful, you know. I would dearly love to have her—"

Constance shook her head. "You're not stealing her."

"Cutting into Constance's wedding celebration and now she's attempting to steal her servants. Is there no end to the outrageous behaviors?" Aldora asked, her expression deadpan.

Emilia drew back, pressing a palm to her chest. "Of course I wouldn't. Not really." The marchioness gave a little toss of her damp curls. "Either way, I'll not let any of you distract me anymore from the importance of this meeting." The marchioness drew in a breath. "Dukes."

The lengthy silence was broken a moment later by more muffled laughter from their respective spouses hiding in the conservatory.

"Uh… I don't suppose you are on that whole business of 'the hearts of dukes' again," Aldora ventured. "I assure you I'm quite content with my Michael."

"This isn't about you, Aldora." Emilia looked to Rowena. "Or you, Rowena. Or you. Or you," she said to Constance and Meredith. "Nearly all of us have won the hearts of dukes or eventual dukes."

"And?" Constance asked, stealing another longing look in her husband's direction.

Emilia pinched her lightly on the arm and then returned to her satchels. Dropping to a knee, she withdrew a stack of...

Constance wrinkled her brow. "Mrs. Matcher's?" She joined her friend on the ground. More specifically... *Five Ways to Win the Heart of a Duke*. That particular column in Mrs. Matcher's had been met with scorn and derision at the sheer scandalous nature of the guidance that had been given to young, unmarried ladies. The column had also proven one of the most successful, selling countless copies.

"I've found as many as I could." Emilia looked up at her friends. "We need to bury them."

"If we were determined that no one should ever see them, wouldn't it make more sense to... burn them?" Rowena asked with her usual pragmatism.

Burn them? That column that only Emilia and Connell knew Constance had written? And yet, so much of Constance's joy had come from these very pages.

"We cannot destroy words, Rowena." Emilia stroked a reverent hand over them. "Especially not these."

"I wrote them," Constance murmured, earning shocked stares from her dearest friends.

Aldora was the first to find her footing. "Well, then we're certainly not destroying them."

"We're not destroying them," Emilia said impatiently. She paused. "We're *hiding* them."

Aldora collected one of the papers. "Hiding them... from *whom?*"

Emilia looked meaningfully at each woman's rounded belly.

And then it made sense. Or at least, Emilia's intentions made sense.

"They'll never find dukes. And worse, they'll be filled with a romantic belief that they should seek out the attentions of those most powerful peers."

"We married those most powerful peers," Constance felt inclined to remind her.

"But it's unrealistic. An impossibility that our daughters will do the same. After all, it's not as though there are endless dukes running about England."

They nodded sagely.

"And it is far more important that our daughters focus on winning the hearts of honorable men without a thought of a title," Aldora said softly.

Emilia beamed. "Precisely."

Constance stared at the massive collection of papers Emilia had managed to gather up that now rested alongside the hole. A pang struck at the idea of those works being buried.

Scooting closer, Emilia caught Constance's hand. "It occurs I've been insensitive," she said softly. "We should keep them. They are your works…"

Constance picked up one of the papers. As much as her friend's intentions stung, there was also a truth to the concerns Emilia had raised. Constance saw that now. She read the title inked upon the front: *Five Ways to Win the Heart of a Duke.*

And yet, for as special as those days had been with Connell, and as true as those lessons, in fact, were, there also remained one inherent error that would mislead young ladies… all women: It didn't matter if it was the heart of a duke but, as Aldora had pointed out, the heart of a man of honor.

Constance nodded and then slowly lowered the paper in her hands into the hole.

"You are… certain?" Emilia asked.

"Yes." Constance held her gaze. "But I would like the opportunity to rewrite the column in the future… to issue a correction where the lessons are laid out to make clear that the only thing that matters is that a lady is winning the heart of a kind, honorable man worthy of her."

Emilia smiled and held her palm out.

A short while later, the collected papers had been filed away into the ground and covered with dirt.

The women stood around, staring at the small mound.

"Our daughters will know that titles matter not at all," Rowena said quietly.

There was a poignancy to that little burial, as they were once more the girls they'd been... ladies united. Only this time, it was born of a different purpose. Constance stared on wistfully. How fast time had passed. Soon, as Emilia had pointed out, their children would be grown... and plotting... and planning in matters of the heart.

"Are you returning with us?" Emilia asked when the group started back for the front of the gardens.

Constance shook her head. "I'll be along shortly."

The door to the conservatory opened, and Connell stepped out. Cupping his hands around his mouth, he called out, "Would it be permissible that I may spend some time with my bride?"

Constance's heart leaped as he approached. The moment he reached her side, she stepped into his arms and lifted her mouth up to his for a kiss.

Her belly fluttered and danced from that tender meeting. When he drew back, Connell glanced down at the earth. "Dare I ask?"

Her lips twitched. "Emilia advised that we bury Mrs. Matcher's *Five Ways to Win the Heart of a Duke.*"

He wrinkled his brow.

"The dearth of dukes, of course."

"Ahh," he said with a mock solemnity. "Of course." That teasing lifted. "And what do you wish?" Connell stroked his knuckles down her cheek, and closing her eyes, she leaned into that softest of touches.

"I..." *Can barely recall my name when you touch me, let alone properly think.*

Constance forced her lids open. "I know that if we have daughters," she began slowly, "I do not want them thinking a title is what matters most, or even at all, when they consider matters of the heart. And yet..."

"And yet?"

A swell of emotion flooded her breast, and she lifted her eyes to his. "And yet, I know that had some young lady not been asking about winning the heart of a duke, then I'd not have had the idea to visit with you those five days, and then... I'd have never known the love that I do."

Connell caressed a palm over her cheek once more. That touch too fleeting as he released her... and... unbuttoned his jacket.

She widened her eyes. "What are you doing?" she whispered, stealing a glance at the empty conservatory. When she looked back, Connell already had his shirt-sleeves rolled up.

He grinned his rogue's grin and grabbed the shovel. "I'll be damned if I see you bury anything you've ever written."

"Even if it gives our future daughters false ideas on matters of the heart?"

His brow dipped. And he faltered. She could all but see his thoughts turning: the fear, the anxiousness.

Connell gave his head a shake and began digging. "We keep the papers for us, then, and we'll teach our children from what we know to be true."

She drifted over. "And what is that, dear husband?"

Holding on to the shovel with one hand, Connell caught Constance about the waist with the other and drew her close. "Love is all they'll need."

Constance looped her arms about his neck and drew herself up onto her toes so their noses almost touched. "And love is what we'll always have."

Connell smiled. "Indeed, we will, my duchess. Indeed, we will."

As he again kissed her, she tasted that promise on his lips. *Forever.*

THE END

COMING SOON

If you enjoyed *Five Days With a Duke*, be sure and read *The Spinster Who Saved a Scoundrel*, the next installment in my *Brethren* series!

In the next *Brethren* installment, a clever spinster is matched with a traitor to the Crown.

The death of her father leaves Miss Francesca Cornworthy .... alone, and with one last wish to fulfill—that she marry a safe, respectable gentleman. She sets herself on a course to honor that request. That is until she crosses paths with Mr. Lathan Holman— the very opposite type of gentleman her father wished her to wed.

After one mistake earned him the title of traitor, Lathan Holman has no interest in reentering society. Then he meets a quick- witted, sharp-mouthed spinster. His dark past clouds his present and future. He'd been certain he'd never laugh or smile again... but it isn't long before, he finds himself doing both with Miss Francesca Cornworthy...and wanting more.

OTHER BOOKS BY
CHRISTI CALDWELL

THE SPINSTER WHO SAVED A SCOUNDREL
Book 5 in the "Brethren" Series by Christi Caldwell

The death of her father leaves Miss Francesca Cornworthy ....
alone, and with one last wish to fulfill—that she marry a safe,
respectable gentleman. She sets herself on a course to honor that
request. That is until she crosses paths with Mr. Lathan Holman—
the very opposite type of gentleman her father wished her to wed.

After one mistake earned him the title of traitor, Lathan Holman
has no interest in reentering society. Then he meets a quick-
witted, sharp-mouthed spinster. His dark past clouds his present
and future. He'd been certain he'd never laugh or smile again…
but it isn't long before, he finds himself doing both with Miss
Francesca Cornworthy…and wanting more.

THE MINX WHO MET HER MATCH"
Book 4 in the "Brethren" Series by Christi Caldwell

Duncan Everleigh, barrister, widower, father. Accused murderer…
Found innocent in the death of his wife, Duncan's reputation is
ruined, his law practice is nearly destroyed, and his daughter hates
him. He's content living for his work. Until one day he meets…

Miss Josephine Pratt…Her life is in tatters. Her oldest brother has brought them to financial ruin. Her betrothed has broken their engagement. Looking to escape, Josephine loses herself in her real passion—her other brother's law books. A chance meeting in the London streets soon finds her employed by the last man she should, the barrister who'll be opposing her brother in court.

Soon, Duncan and Josephine, two people who have vowed to never love again, find the protective walls they've each built, crumbling. When past secrets threaten to destroy their future, they'll have to decide if love is enough.

THE ROGUE WHO RESCUED HER
Book 3 in the "Brethren" Series by Christi Caldwell

Martha Donaldson went from being a nobleman's wife, and respected young mother, to the scandal of her village. After learning the dark lie perpetuated against her by her 'husband', she knows better than to ever trust a man. Her children are her life and she'll protect them at all costs. When a stranger arrives seeking the post of stable master, everything says to turn him out. So why does she let him stay?

Lord Sheldon Graham Whitworth has lived with the constant reminders of his many failings. The third son of a duke, he's long been underestimated: that however, proves a valuable asset as he serves the Brethren, an illustrious division in the Home Office. When Graham's first mission sees him assigned the role of guard to a young widow and her son, he wants nothing more than to finish quickly and then move on to another, more meaningful assignment.

Except, as the secrets between them begin to unravel, Martha's trust is shattered, and Graham is left with the most vital mission he'll ever face—winning Martha's heart.

THE LADY WHO LOVED HIM
Book 2 in the "Brethren" Series by Christi Caldwell

In this passionate, emotional Regency romance by Christi Caldwell, society's most wicked rake meets his match in the clever Lady Chloe Edgerton! And nothing will ever be the same!

She doesn't believe in marriage....

The cruelty of men is something Lady Chloe Edgerton understands. Even in her quest to better her life and forget the past, men always seem determined to control her. Overhearing the latest plan to wed her to a proper gentleman, Chloe finally has enough...but one misstep lands her in the arms of the most notorious rake in London.

The Marquess of Tennyson doesn't believe in love....

Leopold Dunlop is a ruthless, coldhearted rake... a reputation he has cultivated. As a member of The Brethren, a secret spy network, he's committed his life to serving the Crown, but his rakish reputation threatens to overshadow that service. When he's caught in a compromising position with Chloe, it could be the last nail in the coffin of his career unless he's willing to enter into a marriage of convenience.

A necessary arrangement...

A loveless match from the start, it soon becomes something more. As Chloe and Leo endeavor to continue with the plans for their lives prior to their marriage, Leo finds himself not so immune to his wife – or to the prospect of losing her.

THE SPY WHO SEDUCED HER
Book 1 in the "Brethren" Series by Christi Caldwell

A widow with a past... The last thing Victoria Barrett, the Viscountess Waters, has any interest in is romance. When the only man she's ever loved was killed she endured an arranged marriage to a cruel man in order to survive. Now widowed, her only focus is on clearing her son's name from the charge of murder. That is until the love of her life returns from the grave.

A leader of a once great agency... Nathaniel Archer, the Earl of Exeter head of the Crown's elite organization, The Brethren, is back on British soil. Captured and tortured 20 years ago, he clung to memories of his first love until he could escape. Discovering she has married whilst he was captive, Nathaniel sets aside the distractions of love...until an unexpected case is thrust upon him—to solve the murder of the Viscount Waters. There is just one complication: the prime suspect's mother is none other than Victoria, the woman he once loved with his very soul.

Secrets will be uncovered and passions rekindled. Victoria and Nathaniel must trust one another if they hope to start anew—in love and life. But will duty destroy their last chance?

ROGUES RUSH IN
A Regency Duet by Tessa Dare & Christi Caldwell

New York Times and *USA Today* Bestselling authors Tessa Dare and Christi Caldwell come together in this smart, sexy, not-to-be-missed Regency Duet!

Two scandalous brides...
Two rogues who won't be denied...

HIS BRIDE FOR THE TAKING BY NYT BESTSELLING AUTHOR TESSA DARE

It's the first rule of friendship among gentlemen: Don't even think about touching your best friend's sister. But Sebastian, Lord Byrne, has never been one for rules. He's thought about touching Mary Clayton—a lot—and struggled to resist temptation. But when Mary's bridegroom leaves her waiting at the altar, only Sebastian can save her from ruin. By marrying her himself.

In eleven years, he's never laid a finger on his best friend's sister. Now he's going to take her with both hands. To have, to hold... and to love.

HIS DUCHESS FOR A DAY BY USA TODAY BESTSELLER CHRISTI CALDWELL

It was never meant to be...

That's what Elizabeth Terry has told herself while trying to forget the man she married—her once best friend. Passing herself off as a widow, Elizabeth has since built a life for herself as an instructor at a finishing school, far away from that greatest of mistakes. But the past has a way of finding you, and now that her husband has found her, Elizabeth must face the man she's tried to forget.

It was time to right a wrong...

Crispin Ferguson, the Duke of Huntington, has spent the past years living with regret. The young woman he married left without a by-your-leave, and his hasty elopement had devastating repercussions. Despite everything, Crispin never stopped thinking about Elizabeth. Now that he's found her, he has one request—be his duchess, publicly, just for a day.

Can spending time together as husband and wife rekindle the bond they once shared? Or will a shocking discovery tear them apart...this time, forever?

THE VIXEN
Book 2 in the "Wicked Wallflowers" Series by Christi Caldwell

Set apart by her ethereal beauty and fearless demeanor, Ophelia Killoran has always been a mystery to those around her—and a woman they underestimated. No one would guess that she spends her nights protecting the street urchins of St. Giles. Ophelia knows what horrors these children face. As a young girl, she faced those horrors herself, and she would have died…if not for the orphan boy who saved her life.

A notorious investigator, Connor Steele never expected to encounter Ophelia Killoran on his latest case. It has been years since he sacrificed himself for her. Now, she hires orphans from the street to work in her brother's gaming hell. But where does she find the children…and what are her intentions?

Ophelia and Connor are at odds. After all, Connor now serves the nobility, and that is a class of people Ophelia knows firsthand not to trust. But if they can set aside their misgivings and work together, they may discover that their purposes—and their hearts—are perfectly aligned.

THE HELLION
Book 1 in the "Wicked Wallflowers" Series by Christi Caldwell

Adair Thorne has just watched his gaming-hell dream disappear into a blaze of fire and ash, and he's certain that his competitors, the Killorans, are behind it. His fury and passion burn even hotter when he meets Cleopatra Killoran, a tart-mouthed vixen who mocks him at every turn. If she were anyone else but the enemy, she'd ignite a desire in him that would be impossible to control.

No one can make Cleopatra do anything. That said, she'll do

whatever it takes to protect her siblings—even if that means being sponsored by their rivals for a season in order to land a noble husband. But she will not allow her head to be turned by the infuriating and darkly handsome Adair Thorne.

There's only one thing that threatens the rules of the game: Cleopatra's secret. It could unravel the families' tenuous truce and shatter the unpredictably sinful romance mounting between the hellion...and a scoundrel who could pass for the devil himself.

To Tempt a Scoundrel
Book 15 in the "Heart of a Duke" Series by Christi Caldwell

Never trust a gentleman...

Once before, Lady Alice Winterbourne trusted her heart to an honorable, respectable man... only to be jilted in the scandal of the Season. Longing for an escape from all the whispers and humiliation, Alice eagerly accepts an invitation to her friend's house party. In the country, she hopes to find some peace from the embarrassment left in London... Unfortunately, she finds her former betrothed and his new bride in attendance.

Never love a lady...

Lord Rhys Brookfield has no interest in marriage. Ever. He's worked quite hard at building both his fortune and his reputation as a rogue—and intends to enjoy all that they can offer him. That is if his match-making mother will stop pairing him with prospective brides. When Rhys and Alice meet, sparks flare. But with every new encounter, their first impressions of one another are challenged and an unlikely friendship is forged.

Desperate, Rhys proposes a pretend courtship, one meant to spite Alice's former betrothed and prevent any matchmaking attempts toward Rhys. What neither expects is that a pretense can become so much more. Or that a burning passion can heal... and hurt.

BEGUILED BY A BARON
Book 14 in the "Heart of a Duke" Series by Christi Caldwell

A Lady with a Secret… Partially deaf, with a birthmark marring her face, Bridget Hamilton is content with her life, even if she's been cast out of her family. But her peaceful existence—expanding her mind with her study of rare books—is threatened with an ultimatum from her evil brother—steal a valuable book or give up her son. Bridget has no choice; her son is her world.

A Lord with a Purpose… Vail Basingstoke, Baron Chilton is known throughout London as the Bastard Baron. After battling at Waterloo, he establishes himself as the foremost dealer in rare books and builds a fortune, determined to never be like the self-serving duke who sired him. He devotes his life to growing his fortune to care for his illegitimate siblings, also fathered by the duke. The chance to sell a highly coveted book for a financial windfall is his only thought.

Two Paths Collide… When Bridget masquerades as the baron's newest housekeeper, he's hopelessly intrigued by her quick wit and her skill with antique tomes. Wary from having his heart broken in the past, it should be easy enough to keep Bridget at arm's length, yet desire for her dogs his steps. As they spend time in each other's company, understanding for life grows as does love, but when Bridget's integrity is called into question, Vail's world is shattered—as is his heart again. Now Bridget and Vail will have to overcome the horrendous secrets and lies between them to grasp a love—and life—together.

To Enchant a Wicked Duke
Book 13 in the "Heart of a Duke" Series by Christi Caldwell

A Devil in Disguise

Years ago, when Nick Tallings, the recent Duke of Huntly, watched his family destroyed at the hands of a merciless nobleman, he vowed revenge. But his efforts had been futile, as his enemy, Lord Rutland is without weakness.

Until now…

With his rival finally happily married, Nick is able to set his ruthless scheme into motion. His plot hinges upon Lord Rutland's innocent, empty-headed sister-in-law, Justina Barrett. Nick will ruin her, marry her, and then leave her brokenhearted.

A Lady Dreaming of Love

From the moment Justina Barrett makes her Come Out, she is labeled a Diamond. Even with her ruthless father determined to sell her off to the highest bidder, Justina never gives up on her hope for a good, honorable gentleman who values her wit more than her looks.

A Not-So-Chance Meeting

Nick's ploy to ensnare Justina falls neatly into place in the streets of London. With each carefully orchestrated encounter, he slips further and further inside the lady's heart, never anticipating that Justina, with her quick wit and strength, will break down his own defenses. As Nick's plans begins to unravel, he's left to determine which is more important—Justina's love or his vow for vengeance. But can Justina ever forgive the duke who deceived her?

One Winter with a Baron

Book 12 in the "Heart of a Duke" Series by Christi Caldwell

A clever spinster:

Content with her spinster lifestyle, Miss Sybil Cunning wants to prove that a future as an unmarried woman is the only life for her. As a bluestocking who values hard, empirical data, Sybil needs help with her research. Nolan Pratt, Baron Webb, one of society's most scandalous rakes, is the perfect gentleman to help her. After all, he inspires fear in proper mothers and desire within their daughters.

A notorious rake:

Society may be aware of Nolan Pratt, Baron's Webb's wicked ways, but what he has carefully hidden is his miserable handling of his family's finances. When Sybil presents him the opportunity to earn much-needed funds, he can't refuse.

A winter to remember:

However, what begins as a business arrangement becomes something more and with every meeting, Sybil slips inside his heart. Can this clever woman look beneath the veneer of a coldhearted rake to see the man Nolan truly is?

To Redeem a Rake

Book 11 in the "Heart of a Duke" Series by Christi Caldwell

He's spent years scandalizing society.
Now, this rake must change his ways.

Society's most infamous scoundrel, Daniel Winterbourne, the Earl of Montfort, has been promised a small fortune if he can relinquish his wayward, carousing lifestyle. And behaving means he must also help find a respectable companion for his youngest sister—someone who will guide her and whom she can emulate.

However, Daniel knows no such woman. But when he encounters a childhood friend, Daniel believes she may just be the answer to all of his problems.

Having been secretly humiliated by an unscrupulous blackguard years earlier, Miss Daphne Smith dreams of finding work at Ladies of Hope, an institution that provides an education for disabled women. With her sordid past and a disfigured leg, few opportunities arise for a woman such as she. Knowing Daniel's history, she wishes to avoid him, but working for his sister is exactly the stepping stone she needs.

Their attraction intensifies as Daniel and Daphne grow closer, preparing his sister for the London Season. But Daniel must resist his desire for a woman tarnished by scandal while Daphne is reminded of the boy she once knew. Can society's most notorious rake redeem his reputation and become the man Daphne deserves?

To Woo a Widow

Book 10 in the "Heart of a Duke" Series by Christi Caldwell

They see a brokenhearted widow.
She's far from shattered.
Lady Philippa Winston is never marrying again. After her late husband's cruelty that she kept so well hidden, she has no desire to search for love.

Years ago, Miles Brookfield, the Marquess of Guilford, made a frivolous vow he never thought would come to fruition—he promised to marry his mother's goddaughter if he was unwed by the age of thirty. Now, to his dismay, he's faced with honoring that pledge. But when he encounters the beautiful and intriguing Lady Philippa, Miles knows his true path in life. It's up to him to break down every belief Philippa carries about gentlemen, proving that not only is love real, but that he is the man deserving of her sheltered heart.

Will Philippa let down her guard and allow Miles to woo a widow in desperate need of his love?

THE LURE OF A RAKE
Book 9 in the "Heart of a Duke" Series by Christi Caldwell

A Lady Dreaming of Love

Lady Genevieve Farendale has a scandalous past. Jilted at the altar years earlier and exiled by her family, she's now returned to London to prove she can be a proper lady. Even though she's not given up on the hope of marrying for love, she's wary of trusting again. Then she meets Cedric Falcot, the Marquess of St. Albans whose seductive ways set her heart aflutter. But with her sordid history, Genevieve knows a rake can also easily destroy her.

An Unlikely Pairing

What begins as a chance encounter between Cedric and Genevieve becomes something more. As they continue to meet, passions stir. But with Genevieve's hope for true love, she fears Cedric will be unable to give up his wayward lifestyle. After all, Cedric has spent years protecting his heart, and keeping everyone out. Slowly, she chips away at all the walls he's built, but when he falters, Genevieve can't offer him redemption. Now, it's up to Cedric to prove to Genevieve that the love of a man is far more powerful than the lure of a rake.

TO TRUST A ROGUE
Book 8 in the "Heart of a Duke" Series by Christi Caldwell

A rogue

Marcus, the Viscount Wessex has carefully crafted the image of rogue and charmer for Polite Society. Under that façade, however, dwells a man whose dreams were shattered almost eight years earlier by a young lady who captured his heart, pledged her love, and then left him, with nothing more than a curt note.

A widow

Eight years earlier, faced with no other choice, Mrs. Eleanor Collins, fled London and the only man she ever loved, Marcus, Viscount Wessex. She has now returned to serve as a companion for her elderly aunt with a daughter in tow. Even though they're next door neighbors, there is little reason for her to move in the same circles as Marcus, just in case, she vows to avoid him, for he reminds her of all she lost when she left.

Reunited

As their paths continue to cross, Marcus finds his desire for Eleanor just as strong, but he learned long ago she's not to be trusted. He will offer her a place in his bed, but not anything more. Only, Eleanor has no interest in this new, roguish man. The more time they spend together, the protective wall they've constructed to keep the other out, begin to break. With all the betrayals and secrets between them, Marcus has to open his heart again. And Eleanor must decide if it's ever safe to trust a rogue.

To Wed His Christmas Lady
Book 7 in the "Heart of a Duke" Series by Christi Caldwell

She's longing to be loved:

Lady Cara Falcot has only served one purpose to her loathsome father—to increase his power through a marriage to the future Duke of Billingsley. As such, she's built protective walls about her heart, and presents an icy facade to the world around her. Journeying home from her finishing school for the Christmas holidays, Cara's carriage is stranded during a winter storm. She's forced to tarry at a ramshackle inn, where she immediately antagonizes another patron—William.

He's avoiding his duty in favor of one last adventure:

William Hargrove, the Marquess of Grafton has wanted only one thing in life—to avoid the future match his parents would have him make to a cold, duke's daughter. He's returning home from a blissful eight years of traveling the world to see to his responsibilities. But when a winter storm interrupts his trip and lands him at a falling-down inn, he's forced to share company with a commanding Lady Cara who initially reminds him exactly of the woman he so desperately wants to avoid.

A Christmas snowstorm ushers in the spirit of the season:

At the holiday time, these two people who despise each other due to first perceptions are offered renewed beginnings and fresh starts. As this gruff stranger breaks down the walls she's built about herself, Cara has to determine whether she can truly open her heart to trusting that any man is capable of good and that she herself is capable of love. And William has to set aside all previous thoughts he's carried of the polished ladies like Cara, to be the man to show her that love.

THE HEART OF A SCOUNDREL
Book 6 in the "Heart of a Duke" Series by Christi Caldwell

Ruthless, wicked, and dark, the Marquess of Rutland rouses terror in the breast of ladies and nobleman alike. All Edmund wants in life is power. After he was publically humiliated by his one love Lady Margaret, he vowed vengeance, using Margaret's niece, as his pawn. Except, he's thwarted by another, more enticing target—Miss Phoebe Barrett.

Miss Phoebe Barrett knows precisely the shame she's been born to. Because her father is a shocking letch she's learned to form her own opinions on a person's worth. After a chance meeting with the Marquess of Rutland, she is captivated by the mysterious man. He, too, is a victim of society's scorn, but the more encounters she has with Edmund, the more she knows there is powerful depth and emotion to the jaded marquess.

The lady wreaks havoc on Edmund's plans for revenge and he finds he wants Phoebe, at all costs. As she's drawn into the darkness of his world, Phoebe risks being destroyed by Edmund's ruthlessness. And Phoebe who desires love at all costs, has to determine if she can ever truly trust the heart of a scoundrel.

TO LOVE A LORD
Book 5 in the "Heart of a Duke" Series by Christi Caldwell

All she wants is security:

The last place finishing school instructor Mrs. Jane Munroe belongs, is in polite Society. Vowing to never wed, she's been scuttled around from post to post. Now she finds herself in the Marquess of Waverly's household. She's never met a nobleman she liked, and when she meets the pompous, arrogant marquess, she remembers why. But soon, she discovers Gabriel is unlike any gentleman she's ever known.

All he wants is a companion for his sister:

What Gabriel finds himself with instead, is a fiery spirited, bespectacled woman who entices him at every corner and challenges his age-old vow to never trust his heart to a woman. But...there is something suspicious about his sister's companion. And he is determined to find out just what it is.

All they need is each other:

As Gabriel and Jane confront the truth of their feelings, the lies and secrets between them begin to unravel. And Jane is left to decide whether or not it is ever truly safe to love a lord.

Loved By a Duke
Book 4 in the "Heart of a Duke" Series by Christi Caldwell

For ten years, Lady Daisy Meadows has been in love with Auric, the Duke of Crawford. Ever since his gallant rescue years earlier, Daisy knew she was destined to be his Duchess. Unfortunately, Auric sees her as his best friend's sister and nothing more. But perhaps, if she can manage to find the fabled heart of a duke pendant, she will win over the heart of her duke.

Auric, the Duke of Crawford enjoys Daisy's company. The last thing he is interested in however, is pursuing a romance with a woman he's known since she was in leading strings. This season, Daisy is turning up in the oddest places and he cannot help but notice that she is no longer a girl. But Auric wouldn't do something as foolhardy as to fall in love with Daisy. He couldn't. Not with the guilt he carries over his past sins… Not when he has no right to her heart…But perhaps, just perhaps, she can forgive the past and trust that he'd forever cherish her heart—but will she let him?

The Love of a Rogue
Book 3 in the "Heart of a Duke" Series by Christi Caldwell

Lady Imogen Moore hasn't had an easy time of it since she made her Come Out. With her betrothed, a powerful duke breaking it off to wed her sister, she's become the *tons* favorite piece of gossip. Never again wanting to experience the pain of a broken heart, she's resolved to make a match with a polite, respectable gentleman. The last thing she wants is another reckless rogue.

Lord Alex Edgerton has a problem. His brother, tired of Alex's carousing has charged him with chaperoning their remaining, unwed sister about *ton* events. Shopping? No, thank you. Attending the theatre? He'd rather be at Forbidden Pleasures with a scantily clad beauty upon his lap. The task of *chaperone* becomes even more of a bother when his sister drags along her dearest friend, Lady Imogen to social functions. The last thing he wants in his life is a young, innocent English miss.

Except, as Alex and Imogen are thrown together, passions flare and Alex comes to find he not only wants Imogen in his bed, but also in his heart. Yet now he must convince Imogen to risk all, on the heart of a rogue.

MORE THAN A DUKE
Book 2 in the "Heart of a Duke" Series by Christi Caldwell

Polite Society doesn't take Lady Anne Adamson seriously. However, Anne isn't just another pretty young miss. When she discovers her father betrayed her mother's love and her family descended into poverty, Anne comes up with a plan to marry a respectable, powerful, and honorable gentleman—a man nothing like her philandering father.

Armed with the heart of a duke pendant, fabled to land the wearer a duke's heart, she decides to enlist the aid of the notorious Harry, 6th Earl of Stanhope. A scoundrel with a scandalous past, he is the last gentleman she'd ever wed…however, his reputation marks him the perfect man to school her in the art of seduction so she might ensnare the illustrious Duke of Crawford.

Harry, the Earl of Stanhope is a jaded, cynical rogue who lives for his own pleasures. Having been thrown over by the only woman he ever loved so she could wed a duke, he's not at all surprised when Lady Anne approaches him with her scheme to capture another duke's affection. He's come to appreciate that all women are in fact greedy, title-grasping, self-indulgent creatures. And with Anne's history of grating on his every last nerve, she is the last woman he'd ever agree to school in the art of seduction. Only his friendship with the lady's sister compels him to help.

What begins as a pretend courtship, born of lessons on seduction, becomes something more leaving Anne to decide if she can give her heart to a reckless rogue, and Harry must decide if he's willing to again trust in a lady's love.

FOR LOVE OF THE DUKE
*First Full-Length Book in the "Heart of a Duke" Series
by Christi Caldwell*

After the tragic death of his wife, Jasper, the 8th Duke of Bainbridge buried himself away in the dark cold walls of his home, Castle Blackwood. When he's coaxed out of his self-imposed exile to attend the amusements of the Frost Fair, his life is irrevocably changed by his fateful meeting with Lady Katherine Adamson.

With her tight brown ringlets and silly white-ruffled gowns, Lady Katherine Adamson has found her dance card empty for two Seasons. After her father's passing, Katherine learned the unreliability of men, and is determined to depend on no one, except herself. Until she meets Jasper…

In a desperate bid to avoid a match arranged by her family, Katherine makes the Duke of Bainbridge a shocking proposition—one that he accepts.

Only, as Katherine begins to love Jasper, she finds the arrangement agreed upon is not enough. And Jasper is left to decide if protecting his heart is more important than fighting for Katherine's love.

In Need of a Duke
A Prequel Novella to "The Heart of a Duke" Series
by Christi Caldwell

In Need of a Duke: (Author's Note: This is a prequel novella to "The Heart of a Duke" series by Christi Caldwell. It was originally available in "The Heart of a Duke" Collection and is now being published as an individual novella.

~★~

IT FEATURES A NEW PROLOGUE AND EPILOGUE.

Years earlier, a gypsy woman passed to Lady Aldora Adamson and her friends a heart pendant that promised them each the heart of a duke.

Now, a young lady, with her family facing ruin and scandal, Lady Aldora doesn't have time for mythical stories about cheap baubles. She needs to save her sisters and brother by marrying a titled gentleman with wealth and power to his name. She sets her bespectacled sights upon the Marquess of St. James.

Turned out by his father after a tragic scandal, Lord Michael Knightly has grown into a powerful, but self-made man. With the whispers and stares that still follow him, he would rather be anywhere but London…

Until he meets Lady Aldora, a young woman who mistakes him for his brother, the Marquess of St. James. The connection between Aldora and Michael is immediate and as they come to know one another, Aldora's feelings for Michael war with her sisterly responsibilities. With her family's dire situation, a man of Michael's scandalous past will never do.

Ultimately, Aldora must choose between her responsibilities as a sister and her love for Michael.

ONCE A WALLFLOWER, AT LAST HIS LOVE
Book 6 in the Scandalous Seasons Series

Responsible, practical Miss Hermione Rogers, has been crafting stories as the notorious Mr. Michael Michaelmas and selling them for a meager wage to support her siblings. The only real way to ensure her family's ruinous debts are paid, however, is to marry. Tall, thin, and plain, she has no expectation of success. In London for her first Season she seizes the chance to write the tale of a brooding duke. In her research, she finds Sebastian Fitzhugh, the 5th Duke of Mallen, who unfortunately is perfectly affable, charming, and so nicely... configured... he takes her breath away. He lacks all the character traits she needs for her story, but alas, any duke will have to do.

Sebastian Fitzhugh, the 5th Duke of Mallen has been deceived so many times during the high-stakes game of courtship, he's lost faith in Society women. Yet, after a chance encounter with Hermione, he finds himself intrigued. Not a woman he'd normally consider beautiful, the young lady's practical bent, her forthright nature and her tendency to turn up in the oddest places has his interests... roused. He'd like to trust her, he'd like to do a whole lot more with her too, but should he?

A MARQUESS FOR CHRISTMAS
Book 5 in the Scandalous Seasons Series

Lady Patrina Tidemore gave up on the ridiculous notion of true love after having her heart shattered and her trust destroyed by a black-hearted cad. Used as a pawn in a game of revenge against her brother, Patrina returns to London from a failed elopement with a tattered reputation and little hope for a respectable match. The only peace she finds is in her solitude on the cold winter days at Hyde Park. And even that is yanked from her by two little hellions who just happen to have a devastatingly handsome, but coldly aloof father, the Marquess of Beaufort. Something about the lord stirs the dreams she'd once carried for an honorable gentleman's love.

Weston Aldridge, the 4th Marquess of Beaufort was deceived and betrayed by his late wife. In her faithlessness, he's come to view women as self-serving, indulgent creatures. Except, after a series of chance encounters with Patrina, he comes to appreciate how uniquely different she is than all women he's ever known.

At the Christmastide season, a time of hope and new beginnings, Patrina and Weston, unexpectedly learn true love in one another. However, as Patrina's scandalous past threatens their future and the happiness of his children, they are both left to determine if love is enough.

ALWAYS A ROGUE, FOREVER HER LOVE
Book 4 in the Scandalous Seasons Series

Miss Juliet Marshville is spitting mad. With one guardian missing, and the other singularly uninterested in her fate, she is at the mercy of her wastrel brother who loses her beloved childhood home to a man known as Sin. Determined to reclaim control of Rosecliff Cottage and her own fate, Juliet arranges a meeting with the notorious rogue and demands the return of her property.

Jonathan Tidemore, 5th Earl of Sinclair, known to the *ton* as Sin, is exceptionally lucky in life and at the gaming tables. He has just one problem. Well…four, really. His incorrigible sisters have driven off yet another governess. This time, however, his mother demands he find an appropriate replacement.

When Miss Juliet Marshville boldly demands the return of her precious cottage, he takes advantage of his sudden good fortune and puts an offer to her; turn his sisters into proper English ladies, and he'll return Rosecliff Cottage to Juliet's possession.

Jonathan comes to appreciate Juliet's spirit, courage, and clever wit, and decides to claim the fiery beauty as his mistress. Juliet, however, will be mistress for no man. Nor could she ever love a man who callously stole her home in a game of cards. As Jonathan begins to see Juliet as more than a spirited beauty to warm his bed, he realizes she could be a lady he could love the rest of his life, if only he can convince the proud Juliet that he's worthy of her hand and heart.

Always Proper, Suddenly Scandalous
Book 3 in the Scandalous Seasons Series

Geoffrey Winters, Viscount Redbrooke was not always the hard, unrelenting lord driven by propriety. After a tragic mistake, he resolved to honor his responsibility to the Redbrooke line and live a life, free of scandal. Knowing his duty is to wed a proper, respectable English miss, he selects Lady Beatrice Dennington, daughter of the Duke of Somerset, the perfect woman for him. Until he meets Miss Abigail Stone…

To distance herself from a personal scandal, Abigail Stone flees America to visit her uncle, the Duke of Somerset. Determined to never trust a man again, she is helplessly intrigued by the hard, too-proper Geoffrey. With his strict appreciation for decorum and order, he is nothing like the man' she's always dreamed of.

Abigail is everything Geoffrey does not need. She upends his carefully ordered world at every encounter. As they begin to care for one another, Abigail carefully guards the secret that resulted in her journey to England.

Only, if Geoffrey learns the truth about Abigail, he must decide which he holds most dear: his place in Society or Abigail's place in his heart.

Never Courted, Suddenly Wed
Book 2 in the Scandalous Seasons Series

Christopher Ansley, Earl of Waxham, has constructed a perfect image for the *ton*–the ladies love him and his company is desired by all. Only two people know the truth about Waxham's secret. Unfortunately, one of them is Miss Sophie Winters.

Sophie Winters has known Christopher since she was in leading strings. As children, they delighted in tormenting each other. Now at two and twenty, she still has a tendency to find herself in scrapes, and her marital prospects are slim.

When his father threatens to expose his shame to the *ton*, unless he weds Sophie for her dowry, Christopher concocts a plan to remain a bachelor. What he didn't plan on was falling in love with the lively, impetuous Sophie. As secrets are exposed, will Christopher's love be enough when she discovers his role in his father's scheme?

Forever Betrothed, Never the Bride
Book 1 in the Scandalous Seasons Series

Hopeless romantic Lady Emmaline Fitzhugh is tired of sitting with the wallflowers, waiting for her betrothed to come to his senses and marry her. When Emmaline reads one too many reports of his scandalous liaisons in the gossip rags, she takes matters into her own hands.

War-torn veteran Lord Drake devotes himself to forgetting his days on the Peninsula through an endless round of meaningless associations. He no longer wants to feel anything, but Lady Emmaline is making it hard to maintain a state of numbness. With her zest for life, she awakens his passion and desire for love.

The one woman Drake has spent the better part of his life avoiding is now the only woman he needs, but he is no longer a man worthy of his Emmaline. It is up to her to show him the healing power of love.

A Season of Hope
A Danby Novella

Five years ago when her love, Marcus Wheatley, failed to return from fighting Napoleon's forces, Lady Olivia Foster buried her heart. Unable to betray Marcus's memory, Olivia has gone out of her way to run off prospective suitors. At three and twenty she considers herself firmly on the shelf. Her father, however, disagrees and accepts an offer for Olivia's hand in marriage. Yet it's Christmas, when anything can happen...

Olivia receives a well-timed summons from her grandfather, the Duke of Danby, and eagerly embraces the reprieve from her betrothal.

Only, when Olivia arrives at Danby Castle she realizes the Christmas season represents hope, second chances, and even miracles.

"Winning a Lady's Heart"
A Danby Novella

Author's Note: This is a novella that was originally available in A Summons From The Castle (The Regency Christmas Summons Collection). It is being published as an individual novella.

~★~

For Lady Alexandra, being the source of a cold, calculated wager is bad enough...but when it is waged by Nathaniel Michael Winters, 5th Earl of Pembroke, the man she's in love with, it results in a broken heart, the scandal of the season, and a summons from her grandfather – the Duke of Danby.

To escape Society's gossip, she hurries to her meeting with the duke, determined to put memories of the earl far behind. Except the duke has other plans for Alexandra…plans which include the 5th Earl of Pembroke!

TEMPTED BY A LADY'S SMILE
Book 4 in the "Lords of Honor" Series

Richard Jonas has loved but one woman—a woman who belongs to his brother. Refusing to suffer any longer, he evades his family in order to barricade his heart from unrequited love. While attending a friend's summer party, Richard's approach to love is changed after sharing a passionate and life-altering kiss with a vibrant and mysterious woman. Believing he was incapable of loving again, Richard finds himself tempted by a young lady determined to marry his best friend.

Gemma Reed has not been treated kindly by the *ton*. Often disregarded for her appearance and interests unlike those of a proper lady, Gemma heads to house party to win the heart of Lord Westfield, the man she's loved for years. But her plan is set off course by the tempting and intriguing, Richard Jonas.

A chance meeting creates a new path for Richard and Gemma to forage—but can two people, scorned and shunned by those they've loved from afar, let down their guards to find true happiness?

"RESCUED BY A LADY'S LOVE"
Book 3 in the "Lords of Honor" Series

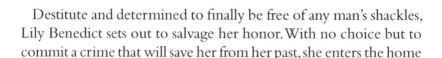

Destitute and determined to finally be free of any man's shackles, Lily Benedict sets out to salvage her honor. With no choice but to commit a crime that will save her from her past, she enters the home of the recluse, Derek Winters, the new Duke of Blackthorne. But entering the "Beast of Blackthorne's" lair proves more threatening than she ever imagined.

With half a face and a mangled leg, Derek—once rugged and charming—only exists within the confines of his home. Shunned by society, Derek is leery of the hauntingly beautiful Lily Benedict. As time passes, she slips past his defenses, reminding him how to live again. But when Lily's sordid past comes back, threatening her life, it's up to Derek to find the strength to become the hero he once was. Can they overcome the darkness of their sins to find a life of love and redemption?

CAPTIVATED BY A LADY'S CHARM
Book 2 in the "Lords of Honor" Series

In need of a wife...

Christian Villiers, the Marquess of St. Cyr, despises the role he's been cast into as fortune hunter but requires the funds to keep his marquisate solvent. Yet, the sins of his past cloud his future, preventing him from seeing beyond his fateful actions at the Battle of Toulouse. For he knows inevitably it will catch up with him, and everyone will remember his actions on the battlefield that cost so many so much—particularly his best friend.

In want of a husband...

Lady Prudence Tidemore's life is plagued by familial scandals, which makes her own marital prospects rather grim. Surely there is one gentleman of the ton who can look past her family and see just her and all she has to offer?

When Prudence runs into Christian on a London street, the charming, roguish gentleman immediately captures her attention. But then a chance meeting becomes a waltz, and now...

A Perfect Match...

All she must do is convince Christian to forget the cold requirements he has for his future marchioness. But the demons in his past prevent him from turning himself over to love. One thing is certain—Prudence wants the marquess and is determined to have him in her life, now and forever. It's just a matter of convincing Christian he wants the same.

ᴄSEDUCED ᴮBY A ᴸLADY'S ᴄHEART
Book 1 in the "Lords of Honor" Series

You met Lieutenant Lucien Jones in "Forever Betrothed, Never the Bride" when he was a broken soldier returned from fighting Boney's forces. This is his story of triumph and happily-ever-after!

~★~

Lieutenant Lucien Jones, son of a viscount, returned from war, to find his wife and child dead. Blaming his father for the commission that sent him off to fight Boney's forces, he was content to languish at London Hospital… until offered employment on the Marquess of Drake's staff. Through his position, Lucien found purpose in life and is content to keep his past buried.

Lady Eloise Yardley has loved Lucien since they were children. Having long ago given up on the dream of him, she married another. Years later, she is a young, lonely widow who does not fit in with the ton. When Lucien's family enlists her aid to reunite father and son, she leaps at the opportunity to not only aid her former friend, but to also escape London.

Lucien doesn't know what scheme Eloise has concocted, but knowing her as he does, when she pays a visit to his employer, he knows she's up to something. The last thing he wants is the temptation that this new, older, mature Eloise presents; a tantalizing reminder of happier times and peace.

Yet Eloise is determined to win Lucien's love once and for all… if only Lucien can set aside the pain of his past and risk all on a lady's heart.

ꟷ𝒪NLY ꟷꟷ𝒪R ꟷꟷEIR ꟷ𝒪VE
Book 3 in the "The Theodosia Sword" Series

Miss Carol Cresswall bore witness to her parents' loveless union and is determined to avoid that same miserable fate. Her mother has altogether different plans—plans that include a match between Carol and Lord Gregory Renshaw. Despite his wealth and power, Carol has no interest in marrying a pompous man who goes out of his way to ignore her. Now, with their families coming together for the Christmastide season it's her mother's last-ditch effort to get them together. And Carol plans to avoid Gregory at all costs.

Lord Gregory Renshaw has no intentions of falling prey to his mother's schemes to marry him off to a proper debutante she's picked out. Over the years, he has carefully sidestepped all endeavors to be matched with any of the grasping ladies.

But a sudden Christmastide Scandal has the potential show Carol and Gregory that they've spent years running from the one thing they've always needed.

ꟷ𝒪NLY ꟷ𝒪R ꟷER ꟷ𝒪NOR
Book 2 in the "The Theodosia Sword" Series

A wounded soldier:
When Captain Lucas Rayne returned from fighting Boney's forces, he was a shell of a man. A recluse who doesn't leave his family's estate, he's content to shut himself away. Until he meets Eve…

A woman alone in the world:
Eve Ormond spent most of her life following the drum alongside her late father. When his shameful actions bring death and pain to English soldiers, Eve is forced back to England, an outcast. With

no family or marital prospects she needs employment and finds it in Captain Lucas Rayne's home. A man whose life was ruined by her father, Eve has no place inside his household. With few options available, however, Eve takes the post. What she never anticipates is how with their every meeting, this honorable, hurting soldier slips inside her heart.

The Secrets Between Them:

The more time Lucas spends with Eve, he remembers what it is to be alive and he lets the walls protecting his heart down. When the secrets between them come to light will their love be enough? Or are they two destined for heartbreak?

ONLY FOR HIS LADY
Book 1 in the "The Theodosia Sword" Series

A curse. A sword. And the thief who stole her heart.

The Rayne family is trapped in a rut of bad luck. And now, it's up to Lady Theodosia Rayne to steal back the Theodosia sword, a gladius that was pilfered by the rival, loathed Renshaw family. Hopefully, recovering the stolen sword will break the cycle and reverse her family's fate.

Damian Renshaw, the Duke of Devlin, is feared by all—all, that is, except Lady Theodosia, the brazen spitfire who enters his home and wrestles an ancient relic from his wall. Intrigued by the vivacious woman, Devlin has no intentions of relinquishing the sword to her.

As Theodosia and Damian battle for ownership, passion ignites. Now, they are torn between their age-old feud and the fire that burns between them. Can two forbidden lovers find a way to make amends before their families' war tears them apart?

MY LADY OF DECEPTION
Book 1 in the "Brethren of the Lords" Series

This dark, sweeping Regency novel was previously only offered as part of the limited edition box sets: "From the Ballroom and Beyond", "Romancing the Rogue", and "Dark Deceptions". Now, available for the first time on its own, exclusively through Amazon is "My Lady of Deception".

~★~

Everybody has a secret. Some are more dangerous than others.

For Georgina Wilcox, only child of the notorious traitor known as "The Fox", there are too many secrets to count. However, after her interference results in great tragedy, she resolves to never help another… until she meets Adam Markham.

Lord Adam Markham is captured by The Fox. Imprisoned, Adam loses everything he holds dear. As his days in captivity grow, he finds himself fascinated by the young maid, Georgina, who cares for him.

When the carefully crafted lies she's built between them begin to crumble, Georgina realizes she will do anything to prove her love and loyalty to Adam—even it means at the expense of her own life.

NON-FICTION WORKS BY
CHRISTI CALDWELL

Uninterrupted Joy: Memoir: My Journey through Infertility, Pregnancy, and Special Needs

The following journey was never intended for publication. It was written from a mother, to her unborn child. The words detailed her struggle through infertility and the joy of finally being pregnant. A stunning revelation at her son's birth opened a world of both fear and discovery. This is the story of one mother's love and hope and…her quest for uninterrupted joy.

BIOGRAPHY

 Christi Caldwell is the bestselling author of historical romance novels set in the Regency era. Christi blames Judith McNaught's "Whitney, My Love," for luring her into the world of historical romance. While sitting in her graduate school apartment at the University of Connecticut, Christi decided to set aside her notes and try her hand at writing romance. She believes the most perfect heroes and heroines have imperfections and rather enjoys tormenting them before crafing a well-deserved happily ever after!

When Christi isn't writing the stories of flawed heroes and heroines, she can be found in her Southern Connecticut home chasing around her eight-year-old son, and caring for twin princesses-in-training!

Visit *www.christicaldwellauthor.com* to learn more about what Christi is working on, or join her on Facebook at Christi Caldwell Author, and Twitter @ChristiCaldwell

Made in the USA
Coppell, TX
26 July 2020

31675482R00118